I0593333

Secrets of River Cottage

A Bindarra Creek Mystery Romance

Annie Seaton

Copyright © 2022 Annie Seaton

ISBN 978-06454381-6-1

Dedication

To Ian, my partner in life and love.

SECRETS OF RIVER COTTAGE

Chapter 1

Cathy Kendall stood on the front porch of River Cottage and fought for calm. Her heart was pounding and the beginning of a migraine tugged at her temples. Closing her eyes, she drew a deep breath and focused on the excited chatter of her two children as they explored the side veranda that led off the porch. For once, the gentle burbling of the river across the paddock failed to calm her churning mind. The heavy sky, threatening imminent rain, reflected her dark and turbulent thoughts.

There was no way she could live in this house again.

No way.

The memories, the fear, and the expectation that her past would finally catch up with her turned her blood to ice. She opened her eyes and took another deep breath as a small hand tugged her arm.

'Mum, this is way cool.' Billy, her twelve-year-old son's voice was filled with excitement. 'Look how close the river is. I can fish all day.'

'You'll be at school all day,' Cathy said, as she put the key in the lock and slowly, reluctantly, pushed open the front door. 'Anyway, it's not certain we'll be living here yet, so don't get too excited. There's still a lot to be decided.'

'Maybe we can go and live at the beach with Nan and Pa, Mummy,' Josie said as she followed Cathy along the hall that ran through the centre of the old house down to the kitchen. 'I don't want them to move away. I'm going to miss them so much.'

'Aw, come on, Mum. What's the problem?' As usual, Billy persisted. 'If we live here, I can fish after school. We can eat what I catch. It would save us some money.'

Josie's little hand snuck into hers as they walked into the kitchen. Cathy ignored the mark on the paint outside the kitchen door,

'It would be a nice house to live in. Look at that stove.' Her small daughter was intuitive and had picked up Cathy's mood, as she always did.

Cathy turned reluctantly to the filthy old combustion stove, and her hand tingled from the memory of an accident long ago.

No, it *hadn't* been an accident. She pushed the thought away as her hand seemed to burn all over again.

'We can bake all sorts of cakes. Do you think it would be all right for sponges?' Her ten-year-old daughter had inherited Cathy's love of baking. 'And there might be duck eggs here too. I saw some ducks at the pond when we drove in. If there are, that would be the absolute icing on the cake!'

Cathy's lips tilted in a smile as Josie parroted one of her nan's sayings. 'It would be, wouldn't it, sweetie? "The icing on the cake", indeed.'

Cathy looked around the kitchen, telling herself it was only a building. She had sat at that red Laminex table when she was in labour with Josie. Billy had been asleep in his bed as she'd waited for Russ to come home from the pub and take her to the hospital. She'd hung on as long as she could after Russ got home so that he'd sobered up enough to look after Billy while she was gone.

It was only bricks and mortar, or in the case of River Cottage, it was half-rotten weatherboards and a rusty roof.

Cathy knew she must put her children first and leave the past behind. The memories weren't embedded in the building; they were in her mind and would follow her wherever they lived. It was time to let go of the past; the move away from Russ's family would be the catalyst for starting afresh, even if they stayed in Bindarra Creek. She still hadn't quite decided if they would stay, but the thought of moving to the city and starting over made her ill.

Russ wasn't here, and he wasn't coming back; that was one of the few certainties in her life. When her in-laws, David and Lea, had announced they were retiring to the coast, Cathy had no inkling that she and the children would have to leave the farm. They'd moved there after Russ had left, and it was the only home Billy and Josie knew. When David told her that they were retiring and Jon, their youngest son, and his wife, Cleo, were moving in to take over the property, Cathy had panicked.

'Oh, sweetheart.' Lea's work-roughened hand had taken Cathy's as she widened her eyes and stared. She knew the colour had left her face by Lea's stricken expression. 'Oh dear, we've handled this all wrong. You know you're like a daughter to us. We'd never abandon you, Cathy,' her mother-in-law said. The words that always remained unspoken hung in the air.

Like our son abandoned you and your children.

Lea and David had been wonderful to them. Cathy had no family, apart from one elderly aunt in Sydney. Her only contact with Aunty Jean was the annual exchange of Christmas cards.

'It's good news and it's exciting for you all,' Lea said. 'We're going to do up River Cottage for you to live in. So much better for Billy and Josie to be in town. They can go to after-school activities, and they won't have that bus trip to town every day.'

'And Mum?' Billy's voice pulled Cathy from her thoughts. 'I can get a kayak and go kayaking across the road with Eddie.'

Cathy frowned. 'Eddie? Who's Eddie?'

'You know, Mum! Eddie Taylor. He's in year eight.'

Cathy nodded. 'Oh yes, Abby and Roman's youngest. I didn't know he was one of your friends.'

'He hangs with us at lunchtime because some of the year eight boys were bullying him about his dad not being his real dad. But I stood up for him. At least *he's* got a dad to do things with.'

Guilt pierced Cathy's chest, but before she could answer, Billy kept talking.

'Anyway, Mum. He's always telling me how much fun it is, and he's invited me out there one day to go for a paddle.'

Cathy frowned. 'Oh, I don't know about that, Billy. That river can be dangerous. You'll have to wait until after all this rain stops. The river is flowing very hard at the moment.'

'Aw, Mum. I can wear a life jacket and anyway, Eddie's dad's in the SES. And now it's getting warmer I can do swimming lessons at the pool. Especially if we're in town. I could go every afternoon.'

Cathy straightened and folded her arms. 'There's a lot to be decided before we start talking swimming lessons and kayaking. This old place needs a lot of work even if we do decide to live here. It's been empty for a long time.'

'Why, Mummy? Is it a bad house? Is that why no one wants to live here?' Josie's face crumpled in a frown, and Cathy hesitated and then crouched in front of her daughter. Josie was small for her age, and along with her intuition came a lot of worries. She was a sensitive little soul, and, like Billy, always took on the more needy children as friends at school. Cathy had tried to shield her children as best she could—depending on who you listened to over the years, the town gossip had had Russ in jail, running away with a bikie gang, and living the high life in Bali.

'No sweetie, it's Nan and Pa's house in town, and they didn't ever rent it out. It's got a bit old, but Pa said they are going to do it up for us *if* we decide to live here.'

'Please, please, please, Mum.' Billy danced around her. 'You could do canteen at school, and we could go for walks along the river, and heaps and heaps of good things.'

'We could have a veggie garden and look, Mum'—Josie stood at the back window—'there's even a chook pen. I can bring Red into town.'

'You and your chooks, Josie!' Cathy forced a smile to her face; she couldn't put the inspection off any longer. 'Come on, let's go and look at the rest of the house and we can think about it. We have plenty of time. Nan and Pa aren't going to the coast until next year.'

Later that afternoon as they turned into the driveway leading to the Kendall farmhouse nestled in the foothills of the Great Dividing Range—not as far out of town as Billy declared—Cathy was surprised to see Jon and Cleo's ute parked near the shed. As far as she knew, they were up north visiting Cleo's parents on their cane farm in North Queensland while Cleo could still fly. Their new baby was due at Christmas.

Cleo was sitting in the sun in the front garden as they opened the gate. Cleo was a beautiful young woman, her lustrous brown curls and dark brown eyes always made Cathy feel old and colourless. But she was a lovely person, and Cathy couldn't ask for a better sister-in-law.

'Hi Cleo, good to see you having a rest for a change.' Cathy put her bag on the table and sat in the chair opposite.

'Lea hunted me out. But it is nice to be sitting out here in the sun.'

'As long as you don't get overheated,' Cathy said.

'Not this spring. It still feels like winter. I am so sick of all the rain,' Cleo said, as one-year-old Benjamin came tottering towards them.

'Oh, Benny's walking. Mum, look!' Josie raced over and held her cousin's hand. 'Clever Benny!'

'Is everything okay? You're back early.' Cathy frowned. 'I thought you were staying up in Queensland for a couple more weeks.'

Cleo reached up and ran a hand through her dark curls. 'Everything's fine, but there's been a slight change in plans. I'll let Lea and David fill you in. What was River Cottage like?'

'Actually, it was nowhere near as bad as I expected. Lea's hired Bridie Bentley to clean it once a month apparently.'

'I thought Bridie left town to live with her daughter after all that stuff out at the Bentley farm a few months ago.'

'No, she seems to have a lot more confidence these days. You see her around town often now. Not that I'm in there that often.' Cathy laughed. 'I've run into her a few times, and she told me Lea has her doing the cleaning. The house is old, but it's liveable.'

'That's good.'

Cathy sent a shrewd glance in Cleo's direction. 'Why do you say that?'

Cleo waved her hand, but a flush stained her fair cheeks. 'Come in, and we'll let David and Lea tell you what's going on.'

Half an hour later, Cathy put her teacup on the table and forced a bright note into her voice. Billy had gone out with David to feed the poddy calf, and Lea was peeling vegetables for dinner. Cleo had taken Benny to the spare room for them both to have a rest.

'So, four weeks, Lea?'

'Yes, and I have so much to do, I don't know where to start.'

'I'll give you a hand. Just tell me anything I can do to help.'

'I still haven't got my head around David changing our plans. When the house sitters let us know they had to leave early, he jumped at the chance of moving to the coast. Wants to go fishing!' Lea shook her head. 'I've got so much on, and it's not long until Christmas. Now I've got to pack up the house and move to the Nambucca Heads house in a month.' She pulled out the chair opposite Cathy and picked up the teapot. 'A top-up, love?'

'Yes, please.' Cathy was still in shock. Once David had explained what was going on, he had asked if she was okay moving into town with the children a few months earlier than planned.

In a month.

When Billy and Josie looked up at her with gleeful anticipation on their faces, she found herself nodding. As well as helping Lea pack up, Cathy knew she had to get herself organised. Not that they really had that much of their own to pack; it was more getting her head around leaving the farm they'd lived on for almost ten years.

'David is going to ring Ryan Rossiter to take a look at the cottage,' Lea said. 'Also, I heard Dodge and Tessa are just back from a trip out west with a truckload of furniture from garage sales. Apparently, they're having a sale to make room in their shop. You might pick up some pieces for the house. If you see anything, we'll pay for it.'

Cathy shook her head. 'No, Lea. It's about time I stood on my own two feet. You and David took us in when Russ . . . when Russ left, and you've been incredibly good to us. I need to make a home for Billy and Josie. I've been thinking of looking for some work in town; there could be a part-time clerical job coming up at the high school. Jaclyn finishes her maternity leave after Christmas, and I know I'd have a pretty good chance of getting the job.' Cathy smiled. 'Even though you left big shoes to fill there.'

Lea's eyes glinted with unshed tears. 'You don't have to work, you know that, Cathy. It was our son who let you down so badly, and looking after you and the kids financially is the least we can do to make amends.'

Cathy reached out and touched her mother-in-law's hand. 'You and David don't have to make amends, you know. You've looked after us for long enough. I truly appreciate what you've done for us, but it's time I learned to be a bit more independent.'

Lea gripped Cathy's hand. 'I just wish we knew what happened to Russ. Is my boy still alive? I guess I have to accept he's not, because if he was, he wouldn't have stayed away this long, would he?' Tears rolled down Lea's cheeks. 'I'll never know.'

Cathy kept her thoughts on that to herself as she always had. She reached up and wiped the tears from Lea's face. 'Come on, let's think about something happy. You don't want to end up with a migraine.'

Lea smiled through her tears. 'I certainly don't have time for that at the moment.'

As Cathy searched for a happier topic, Josie came in from the sunroom where she'd been reading. Josie spent most of her time with her head in a book, and had a vivid imagination.

'Don't cry, Nan. Aunty Cleo let me feel her new baby kick in her tummy before. I think she's going to be a soccer player.'

Lea held her arms out and Josie sat on her lap, her little fingers wiping Lea's cheeks as Cathy's had. 'And Aunty Cleo asked me for some ideas for our new baby's name too.'

Cathy smiled at her daughter as she looked across at her. In less than a minute, Josie had Lea distracted and smiling. Her heart clenched as she realised that Lea and David would be a few hundred kilometres away soon. Lea could be difficult to live with at times, but she had been wonderful to Cathy and the children. Since Lea had retired, she had been a lot more giving. Lea calmed as Josie spoke to her, but Cathy was at a loss with the Russ issue as she had been for the past ten years.

What could you say to a mother whose child had disappeared of his own accord? Cathy couldn't imagine what that would be like. She prayed that neither of the children had Russ's temperament.

There was so much that Lea didn't know about her son.

And Cathy would never tell her.

Chapter 2

Two weeks later

Grant Cummings stayed in Tamworth overnight so he could get to Bindarra Creek early the next morning. When he chose the most expensive motel in town, he knew he was making a statement—even if only to himself—a statement that these days he could afford the best. Despite being much older and wiser than he'd been when he'd fled from Bindarra Creek eighteen years ago, Grant couldn't help the nervous tension settling in his gut when he passed the sign telling him the town was only five kilometres ahead. He lifted his foot from the accelerator and the RAM slowed as he took notice of his surroundings. It had been a wet spring; the paddocks were lush and green, and the cattle were fat and shiny.

When he'd been seventeen, Grant hadn't noticed anything about the town or the landscape; all he'd wanted to do was get out of what he called a hick town. To be fair, his years growing up in Bindarra Creek had been mostly happy. In those days, kids could run free. He'd spent his afternoons and weekends outside, playing cricket in the summer and rugby league in the winter. He'd done okay at school, but his enthusiasm for sport had meant little homework had been done. His parents and Sally, his sister, moved to Melbourne a year after he'd left home.

His year ten teacher, Ian Kendall, had written on his final report: "Grant will never make anything of his life until he learns to focus and improves his handwriting."

Grant hoped the old bugger was still in town to see what he *had* made of his life. He would have been better off writing: "Grant will never make anything of his life until he learns to focus and stays away from Russell Kendall."

But back in those days, no one else had seen Russ for what he was, and Grant had been sucked in like the rest of the kids who looked up to Russ. The others had gradually drifted away, and Grant had spent his time at Bindarra Creek High under Russ's influence.

As he approached the outskirts of town, Grant looked to the right to see if the garage was still there. He'd hoped to come across a service centre on the highway, but there hadn't been one. In those characterless centres, you could remain anonymous, although he doubted that anyone would link him to the young thug who'd left town at seventeen.

He pulled in, filled up his tank and paid by credit card to a disinterested teenager who was flicking through her phone. Nothing changes, he thought.

As he drove toward his temporary home, Grant glanced at the swimming pool. It was easy to let his mind go back and remember the summer afternoons he'd spent there in his teens, in awe of Russ and how the girls seemed to find him irresistible. The coconut aroma of Reef Oil, greasy chips and Pluto Pups from the pool shop came to him as though it was only yesterday that he and Russ were showing off to the girls, seeing who could outperform the other with dangerous dives into the deep end of the pool. He turned his gaze back to the road.

The primary and high schools were back down to the right, but he had no desire to revisit the school either. To be honest, Grant had no desire to be in Bindarra Creek, but the information that he'd been given three months ago had started him on a path from which there was no turning back. The only way he could follow that path to his desired conclusion was to settle here and become a respected—if temporary—resident of Bindarra Creek.

The town he'd sworn he would never come back to. He'd been smart enough to get out before he'd got into too much trouble. He'd grown up enough in his senior years to see the bad influence that Russ Kendall and his main offsider, Mike Potter, were having on him. He disagreed with so many things that they did, but Mike had been such a thug, even as a weedy kid, Russ had hung around. Until they'd insisted that he helped them on a job.

Grant had packed up and left town. He had no intention of spending his life in prison, which is what he was certain Russ and Mike were destined for.

Focusing on the familiar streets and not having to think about where he was going, he turned into Willow Drive and headed towards Main Street. His appointment with Hunter Sullivan was at ten o'clock, and he'd just have time to grab a coffee first. He parked the car outside the pharmacy; it hadn't changed one bit. He'd swear that it was the same display that had been in the front window the day he left town. Faded purple fabric provided the same backdrop for the goods on display.

Maybe he was letting his prejudices about Bindarra Creek colour his view. Grant took himself to task; if he continued like this, he was sure to say the wrong thing sooner than later and he couldn't afford to do that.

When he was a kid, there'd been a café up the street towards the river, so he headed that way.

If there wasn't one there now, he'd ask someone where he could find a decent coffee; he'd come a long way since hanging around at the Cyprus Café drinking lime spiders and chocolate milkshakes. The café name came back to him; he hadn't thought of it for years. These days Grant knew and loved his coffee. A cosmopolitan now returned to his roots in an old-fashioned country town, where he figured he'd be lucky if he could find an instant coffee. He threw a glance at the stock and station agency as he walked past, but his attention was taken by the café that was on the other side of it.

The Levonis family had owned the Cyprus Café when he was there, and like the pharmacy, it looked much the same now as it had then, except for some newer tables on the footpath outside. A couple of older women sitting at the table closest to the road looked up and smiled at him, as he paused outside the door.

'Best coffee in town, if you're after coffee, dear.'

He turned to the table and recognised them both immediately: Mrs Lette and Mrs Brown. They looked no different, but there was no recognition on either of their faces.

'Thank you,' he said with a quick nod and headed into the café.

A young man with curly dark hair greeted

him with a friendly smile and took his order of an espresso.

'Coming right up, sir.'

Grant raised his eyebrows. Seemed like Bindarra Creek had caught up with the times a bit.

A few minutes later he walked out of the café, holding his takeaway coffee. The two women had gone, so he sat at the table and watched the activity in the street as he waited for ten o'clock to roll around. The town was busier than he remembered; the street had filled since he'd parked and there were quite a few pedestrians walking up each side of the street and crossing the road.

No one paid him any attention, and he quickly finished his coffee—an excellent brew— and stood and put the disposable cup in the bin on the footpath. His tension had eased slightly as he made his way back to the stock and station agency. He wasn't pleased when he saw Mrs Lette and Mrs Brown standing outside looking at the ads in the window, and he wondered if they had expected him to come back this way.

He shook himself mentally; he was being paranoid. Even if they did recognise him, he was just another past resident calling through town. Anyway, as soon as he gave his name somewhere, someone would be sure to connect him with the Cummings who had left town almost twenty years ago.

The two women ignored him as he pushed open the door of the agency and walked across to the desk where a young woman frowned at her computer screen. As his shadow fell across the desk, she looked up.

'Good morning, sir. How may I help you?'

The door opened behind Grant as she spoke, but he didn't turn around.

'Hi there. I have a ten a.m. appointment with Hunter Sullivan. I'm Grant Cummings.'

'I knew I recognised you!' The voice behind him was triumphant.

Grant turned slowly to see a satisfied expression on the face of one of the women who'd been at the café. She'd followed him inside.

'You're Sandra Cummings' son,' she said. He thought she was Mrs Lette; he'd always got them mixed up when he was a teenager, so he took a guess.

'Mrs Lette?' he asked politely.

'Yes, Edwina Lette. Welcome home. Are you here to stay?' she asked bluntly.

Grant looked apologetically at the young woman at the reception desk. 'Excuse me a moment.' He turned to the elderly woman. 'You'll have to excuse me. I have an appointment. It's been a pleasure seeing you again.' Grant knew his bland tone belied his words, but he didn't intend to share his plans with anyone. If she thought he was rude, he didn't care. He owed this town nothing.

'Come on in, Grant. Good to meet you.' Hunter Sullivan was waiting behind him with his hand outstretched. Grant shook it and followed Hunter into the office, and waited for him to shut the door.

'Have a seat,' Hunter said, going to the other side of the desk. 'Another Bindarra Creek boy come home?'

Grant forced a chuckle. 'I don't know that I'd call it home. We moved around a lot when I was a kid, and I didn't live here long. I'm not here to stay this time either. I'm just seeing if it's worth establishing a branch of my business here.'

'Ah, when you built those two apartments, I thought you must have been planning to settle. You could do worse, mate. It's a damn good place to live.'

'No, just an investment property.'

Hunter opened the drawer in his desk and pulled out a set of keys. 'I've had the keys to the duplex here since Ryan finished it. Have you been past it yet?'

'No, I just hit town, grabbed a coffee and came straight here.'

Hunter nodded. 'How long will you stay?'

Grant shrugged as he reached for the keys. 'As long as it takes.'

'You'll have to catch up with some of the guys you went to school with. You'd be surprised how many of us are still around. I think you were in my brother, Reid's year. You were a rugby league player, weren't you? They used to call you Gee?'

'I played one season before we left town.' All Grant hoped was that the years had blurred some memories.

'Reid manages the family property, *Tulachmhor* with our dad. And you'd remember Jake Morgan too? He lives out that way. I'll get them all to come into the pub one night. Be good to have a catch-up.'

Grant put his hands up. 'Look, I'm not here to stay, mate. I'll be coming and going. I've got businesses in a few towns now, so I won't be settling in Bindarra Creek.'

'Fair enough.' Hunter took the hint and turned to the business in hand. He reached for a folder on the side of the desk. 'Here's the lease for the land and the shed on Mt Ingalls Rd. I just need a signature in a couple of places and it's all right to go.'

Grant signed in the two places Hunter indicated.

'Your deposit came in yesterday and the

bond has been put in our trust account. You've still got the account number for the monthly lease payment?'

Grant nodded. 'The direct deposit's been set up already.'

'Good.' Hunter nodded. 'Just one more thing.'

Tension crawled up Grant's spine and into his shoulders. He lifted his hand and rubbed the side of his neck, willing himself to relax. He'd known it was going to be hard, but everyone seemed to remember him. He'd been in town half an hour and it was obvious he wasn't going to be able to keep as low a profile as he wanted to.

That was the problem with small bloody towns. Everyone knew you, and your business, and what they didn't know, they made up.

'Yes?' He knew his voice was clipped, but maybe Hunter would pick up he wasn't here to socialise. If it got around that Grant Cummings was a rude bastard, maybe he'd be left alone. At least until he'd done what he'd come to do, and he could get the hell out of here again.

'Are you looking for staff?' Hunter asked.

'I will be down the track. Eventually, a manager. Why do you ask?'

'I know a few good blokes who are looking for work. They've been made redundant at the council. Outdoor workers, so if you're looking, let me know.'

'Thanks. I will.'

Grant stood and shook Hunter's hand. 'Thanks for handling that for me. Appreciate it.'

'My pleasure. And don't forget, if you want that beer, give me a call.' He picked up a business card and handed it to Grant. 'Any time.'

Grant nodded and didn't look back as he left the agency. At least the two old biddies hadn't waited for him to come out. The street was empty as he jumped into his ute and headed for his new duplex in Court Street.

He couldn't help smiling at the irony of being opposite the police station. At least the old sarge, Trevor Bartlett, who knew him well in those days, would be long gone.

Or Grant hoped he would.

Chapter 3

'Hi, Jaclyn. Sorry, I'm a bit late.' Cathy pulled out the chair on the footpath outside the Cyprus Café and sat opposite Jaclyn Rossiter. She and Jaclyn had become friends after meeting at an RFS social night a few months ago. Lea had dragged Cathy into town that night, telling her she needed to spend more time with people her own age; Cathy and Jaclyn had struck up a friendship. A weekly coffee date had developed from that first meeting, and Cathy was gradually learning to relax a little more each time she came to town.

'It's okay. I haven't been here long. I had some chores to do in town, but I decided to have coffee first. I've ordered the usual for you too.'

'Where's that gorgeous baby of yours today?' Cathy put her bag on the spare chair.

'Georgia is having her first day by herself at daycare,' Jaclyn said, with a sniff. 'And I'm one of those mothers that I used to watch go to pieces when they brought their kids to school on the very first day. Would you believe I cried when I dropped her off?'

'Of course, you did. You're a mother. I

know exactly what it's like. I'll never forget Billy's first day at kindy. And then Josie's.'

Cathy looked over Jaclyn's shoulder as a car drove past the café. Letting the kids out of her sight back then had been hard. Even on the rare occasions she'd left them at the farm with Lea, she'd seen shadows in every corner. It was still hard these days and living in town would mean that they would want to go to other kids' places to play. Billy had already started on that.

'So, tell me what's happening at River Cottage. I hear the move's getting close,' Jaclyn said.

'Yes, it is. We're moving next week.'

'It'll be good for you to be in town, Cathy.'

'I'm still not sure, you know,' Cathy admitted. 'I thought about moving to the city seeing we had to move, you know.'

'That would have been a big move. Plus, huge for the kids too.' Jaclyn looked at her curiously. 'But if that's what you want?'

'No, I wanted to stay out at the farm, but that's selfish, I know. I'm a coward, Jac. I couldn't cope with such a big move. The thought of the city made me shiver. Anyway, we're staying in town.'

'They've sure got that cottage done quickly. I couldn't believe when Ryan said the interior was almost done.'

Cathy nodded. 'I couldn't believe how quickly they did it either. I'm sure Ryan pulled some strings and managed to get some builders to come over from Tamworth. He and Joe have replaced all the rotten weatherboards and I hear the new roof's going on tomorrow.'

'Ryan's really chuffed with the result,' Jaclyn said.

'The painters have been through and there's new carpet in the three bedrooms, and it just looks incredible.'

Jaclyn tipped her head to the side and her soft blonde hair fell around her face. 'So why are you arguing about a new stove?'

Cathy laughed. 'You know me, Jac.'

'I do know you, love. So, it's ready for you to move in?'

'It is. Lea and David are going down to the coast next week. I'm going to spend this week helping Lea finish the last of the packing. Cleo is too. I'll be glad to move in finally.' Cathy rolled her eyes as she put her hands on the table and looked down at her chipped fingernails.

'Gosh, what on earth have you been doing?' Jaclyn asked.

'I've been trying to scrub the old stove in the kitchen at the cottage. Lea wants to buy a new one, but I told her there's nothing wrong with the combustion one.' Cathy chuckled. 'Once I got the rat droppings out anyway.'

'Oh, yuk. Ryan told me it was in a bit of a mess.'

'It's okay now. Your husband is a godsend. I can't believe how quickly he and his brother get work done.'

'Yes, he's really happy that Joe's offered to stay in town. He's got a lot of work lined up, and Joe fits in with his schedule. There's not a lot of shearing after the recent floods.' Jaclyn looked up and smiled at Mrs Levonis as she put their coffee on the table. 'Thank you, Thea.'

'My pleasure, ladies. Now if you decide to have some morning tea, I have a freshly-baked honey cake inside.'

Cathy and Jaclyn looked at each other and laughed when they both nodded at the same time. 'Why not!'

Thea smiled and hurried back into the café, returning almost immediately with two slices of cake covered in whipped cream.

'That smells wonderful,' Cathy said.

Jaclyn reached for the fork and sampled hers. 'It's divine. Now, Cathy, tell me why you won't let Lea and David put a new stove in?'

'Because they're doing too much for me as it is.' Cathy looked down at her hands. 'I just feel bad about them doing so much.'

'Cathy, you have to realise that Billy and Josie are their grandchildren. Of course, they care about them and want to see them in a decent house. I know how much Lea hated telling you that they were moving. You're like a daughter to them. Let them help when they want to.'

'I feel guilty. I should be pulling my weight. I actually found a new duplex in town that I could rent, but by the time I worked up the courage to ask about it, Hunter said it wasn't available.'

'You mean the one Ryan built in Court Street?'

'Yes. Opposite the police station.'

'Ryan was telling me it's actually the owner who's moving in there, and he's decided not to rent the second one out yet. He's the guy who's developing the landscaping business down near the nursery.'

'I think he's the one who's going to build the new fence and put the garden boxes in at the cottage.'

'I didn't think he was in town yet,' Cathy said.

'Ryan said he's due to start work soon. I guess you'll want everything finished before you move in.'

'I was hoping it would be, but David has

decided to get a deck built on the back so we can have somewhere to sit outside. We'll move in before they start that though, I think.'

'A deck, and you said no to a stove? Think of the resale value for them.' Jaclyn looked innocent, but Cathy didn't fall for it.

'If I'm totally honest, the old stove didn't come up that clean, so I guess I'll have to give in and accept the new one.'

'Good. And you do know they care about you too, not just the kids, don't you?'

'I know. I've been very lucky. It's going to be very different living in town by ourselves.' Cathy nodded and smiled at Jaclyn. 'But I'm determined to make a good life for the kids.'

'Now that you're going to be in town, have you thought about looking for a job?'

Cathy lifted her eyes and looked at Jaclyn who was staring at her intently.

'Why do you ask?'

'Because since Lea left the school, there's been a couple of casual administrative officers at the school and now the position is going to an advertisement.'

'Wouldn't it be offered as a transfer first?' Cathy knew how the school system worked from Lea working there. 'If there's a permanent position, I mean.'

'Yes. I know you understand how it works and that's why I want to ask you whether you're interested. There's nobody on the transfer list who has Bindarra Creek on their list of schools so now that the position has been vacated, it will go to ad. I don't know if Lea told you she was still on long service leave. But now she's officially retired so the position's coming up, and I'll get to fill it.'

'So advertised?' Cathy said.

'Yes, and I'd be really pleased if you applied for it. I'm not promising anything as you know the best applicant will get the job, but I think it would be good if you applied. It won't start until after the Christmas holidays though.'

Cathy smiled. 'I was actually talking to Lea about it and said I was going to come and see you about a casual position. I've got secretarial experience, but not in schools. I've kept up with my computer skills. I've had quite a number of remote jobs over the past few years.'

'That's good. The only thing is, how would you feel about working full-time and on-site?'

'It *would* be different for me. And to be honest, I have been a bit of a recluse, so I think it would be good for me to work with others.'

'It would. Even if the school position doesn't come off, there're a few places in town that would snap you up.'

'I don't know about that.'

'Cathy, you undervalue yourself. Working in a team would be good for you.'

Cathy frowned. 'How do you mean?'

'For your confidence. And I hope we're good enough friends that you don't take that the wrong way. You've lived a quiet life out there on the farm.'

Hurt lodged in Cathy's chest. Was that how people saw her? She forced herself to sound confident.

'I won't take offence. All I've wanted is for the kids to have a happy life and be well provided for. And being on the farm has given us that. Having a job will let me be a little bit independent, maybe, and the extra money would be really helpful.'

'And what about *your* happiness?' Jaclyn picked up her cup and then put it down again, hesitating before she spoke. 'Tell me if I'm talking out of line, but with me going back to school, and now having Billy there in the student body, I don't want to say the wrong thing. I don't want to jeopardise our friendship, Cathy.'

'Say the wrong thing? What do you mean? About us living here in town? Or about me getting a job at the school? I don't want to make things difficult for you with us being friends if I do apply when it comes up.'

'You won't be. It's a small town and a small district. I'm likely to know everyone who applies when it's advertised.'

'So, what did you mean about our friendship?'

Jaclyn pushed the empty cake plate to the centre of the table. Cathy still hadn't touched hers. Their conversation had stressed her a little, and her stomach was churning.

'I know you're a very private person, Cathy, and I respect that. I know you're alone. May I ask what happened to your husband? Why you've been living out there?'

Cathy's hand shook as she picked up her cake fork, trying to appear calm. 'My husband? Russ? We were never married. I took his name for the kids.' She cut off a piece of cake and lifted it to her mouth, surprised by the sour flavour of the cake. Her stomach roiled again.

Jaclyn nodded.

'We were living at River Cottage when I was pregnant with Josie. Russ disappeared a month after she was born. Billy was two.' Her voice was flat.

'Disappeared?' Jaclyn said quietly.

'Yes, Russ went out one Friday night and never came home.'

Chapter 4

Grant Cummings parked his RAM on the side road and walked around the back of the cottage. As he approached the building site, a labourer worked the ground with a crowbar. The rain had been consistent since the end of winter and the ground was soft. Since the end of last week when Grant had arrived in town and moved into his apartment, the weather had cleared, and he and Ryan Rossiter had organised an onsite meeting at River Cottage at ten o'clock today.

It looked like work had already started on the footings for the deck that was being added to the back of the small cottage.

'Good to see the sun out, mate,' the young guy commented as Grant walked towards him. The young guy put the crowbar down and held out his hand. 'I guess you're the landscaper? I'm Joe Rossiter, Ryan's brother. He's gone down to the produce store to pick up a few bags of concrete.'

Grant took the proffered hand and shook it. The young man had a firm grip, and his smile was welcoming. 'Grant Cummings.'

'Welcome to Bindarra Creek. I hear you've moved into the new duplex we built.' He chuckled.

'I mean that Ryan built. I'm just the navvie.'

'Thanks, Joe. Yes, and it's good to be settled in. A handy base in town.'

'You're starting a landscaping business,' Joe said as he reached for the crowbar again. 'Are you just setting it up or have you moved to Bindarra Creek to stay?'

Grant hesitated. He'd thought long and hard about his story and had decided to keep it simple. 'Yes, I could see there was an opportunity for a business here. Lots of building going on, and it seemed like a decent enough town to live in. Close to Tamworth for supplies. Time will tell, though, whether I stay or not.'

'Don't worry, Grant. You'll be kept plenty busy. Locals have had to get a company out of Tamworth for their fencing and gardens up until now. There'll be a lot of work available with all the new houses being built out on Mt Ingalls Road.' He chuckled. 'Sorry, I tend to run off at the mouth. I'm sure you did your homework before you moved here. It's not a bad place to live. Bit quiet for me socially, but there's plenty of work.'

Grant nodded and turned when a white Toyota ute pulled up behind his. The cottage was situated in a good position on a double block on the corner of River Street close to Mt Ingalls Road. Grant had gone for a walk last night—River Cottage was only a hundred metres up Court Street from his apartment. He'd scoped the property in the semi-darkness. Nothing much had changed since he'd lived in town. The caravan park across the road backing onto the Akuna River had been there for as long as he could remember. A few permanents still lived there, but not many caravans used it these days from what he could see. The SES headquarters was one block up the road next door to the St Ignatius vicarage, and on the other side of the caravan park, paddocks fronted River Road.

The house on the paddock side of River Cottage had been in darkness and appeared to be empty, and the two blocks behind it hadn't been built on yet. It was quite a secluded and private residential block. Shouldn't be too hard to suss out one night. If anyone saw him around, he had the excuse of being the landscaper for the owner.

'That's Ryan now,' Joe said. 'I'd better get back to work.'

Grant walked over to the ute as a tall, broad-shouldered guy hefted a bag of concrete onto his shoulder from the tray at the back of the ute. 'Hi there. Want a hand? I'm Grant Cummings.'

'Thanks, Grant, appreciate it. I thought it must have been your RAM. Great ute.'

'I'm pretty happy with it.' Grant reached across the tray of Ryan's ute and dragged a bag of concrete over. He lifted it to his shoulder and walked across to the small shed next to a chook run in the backyard of the block.

'It's been so wet, we're using the old shed to store all the building stuff,' Ryan said. He wiped his hand on his work trousers and held it out. 'Good to finally meet you, Grant. Welcome to town.'

'Ditto, mate. It's good to meet you too. I have to say thanks for being so easy to work with by phone when you were building the duplex for me.'

'You're happy with it?'

'Very. You've done a top job. Once I get a bit of landscaping done around the front, it'll be great.'

'Are you going to settle there or is it just a temporary base for you?' Ryan asked. 'I know how much you were travelling around when we were building the duplex. You seemed to be in a different town every time we spoke.'

'I'll stay for a while. I've got the business in town to get up and running. I'll be hiring in the next few weeks if you can recommend someone.'

'Labour?'

Grant shook his head. 'No, mainly someone to man the office to start with. I'm leasing the block next door to Bindarra Downs nursery.'

'Great, I hadn't heard that. It's a good block

and it'll be a good worksite for you. Plenty of room for earthmoving equipment, and close to the nursery when people come in to buy plants. You'll need a big sign up there, plus one on your ute as you drive around town. It's the best way to get noticed out here.' Ryan chuckled. 'Although the Bindarra Creek grapevine is pretty good.'

Grant nodded. 'I can imagine. Small towns, hey?' He didn't let on that he knew exactly how good the local grapevine was. It had got him into enough trouble when he'd been a teenager. Although to be honest, he'd chosen the company he kept himself. Then he thought about it; the grapevine was so good it wouldn't be long before the old biddies told someone who he was, and maybe Ryan would think it was strange he hadn't mentioned it.

'Nothing changes. I lived here for a while when I was at high school,' he added.

'I'm a blow-in,' Ryan replied, without asking for details. 'Both my wife, Jaclyn, and me, we came from the city. Or rather I came via the city. Grew up in Werris Creek and moved to Sydney to do my construction degree.'

'Construction management?'

Ryan nodded. 'Yep, but I much prefer doing the smaller building work. I came out here to oversee the refurbishment of the high school and I met up with Jac again. She was the principal at the high school. We'd been together for a while in Sydney, but we'd sort of lost touch. Actually, she still is principal, but she's on maternity leave.' Ryan stared into the distance and was quiet for a second or two. Grant sensed there was a bit of a story there. No doubt he'd hear it on the town grapevine eventually.

'Long story short,' Ryan continued. 'We sorted out our problems, married, moved out to Rossiter's Run, a place I'd bought, and now we have Georgia.'

'Sounds like you've settled here,' Grant commented, pleased that the conversation hadn't stayed on him.

'Yeah.' Ryan grinned. 'Turned out that the property I bought had actually been in my family about fifty years back. I was interested in it because it was called Rossiter's Run. It belonged to my birth father's family so I came full circle. You'll have to come out for a beer one night.'

'I'd like that,' Grant said. And he meant it. Ryan Rossiter seemed like a decent bloke. And being a recent arrival, he knew none of Grant's past history. He wondered if Hunter Sullivan had mentioned him to Reid, or Jake Morgan yet. They were the ones he had to keep his distance from.

'Enough about me. Come and I'll show you

what we've done to the cottage, and then you can let me know your schedule. We won't be long with this deck if the weather stays clear. Then we'll be out of your way. Just have this deck to finish, build new back stairs and a bit of work in the kitchen.'

Grant stood back and drew an imaginary line in his head between the corner post of the fence and the third section of the old paling fence. 'How far out is the deck going to go?'

He'd have to follow through with his plan as soon as he could if the deck was going to extend past the third post in the side fence. If Joe was going to be digging too much wider, Grant knew he had to be quick. He'd have to have a look sooner than later.

'That's the perimeter where Ryan has the string line. We'll probably get this done by the end of the week,' Ryan replied.

'Fair enough.' Grant nodded. 'Do you know when the tenants are moving in?'

Ryan pointed to a small red sedan that had pulled up behind his ute. 'Here's Lea and Cathy now. You can ask them.'

Chapter 5

Ryan had rung Lea last night to ask them to come in and have a look at an idea he'd had for the kitchen renovation. Lea said it was up to Cathy but when she mentioned it to her over dinner, Cathy insisted that Lea go into town and make the decision. They'd come head-to-head as they seemed to be doing more frequently lately.

'It's *your* cottage, Lea. It belongs to you and David. I'm just the tenant.'

Lea pursed her lips, and Cathy knew she'd upset her mother-in-law—again—but she was determined to stand on her own two feet this time. She held firm until after they'd cleared the table and washed up.

The silent treatment from Lea was difficult to take. Finally, Cathy relented. Even though Lea was difficult, Cathy knew her stubbornness wasn't easy to live with either.

'I have to take the kids to school tomorrow morning because Josie has to take her costume for the school Christmas play rehearsal and she doesn't want to take it on the bus. Why don't you come in with me and then we can have a look at the house and then have coffee at the café afterwards.'

Lea's mood changed immediately at the peace offering, and she'd been ready to leave this morning before Billy and Josie had even had breakfast.

Cathy sighed and hurried them along. After they dropped the kids off at the primary and high schools, Cathy drove towards River Cottage. She was still nervous about moving there—it didn't feel right, but she'd accepted they would move there until she could find an alternative. As much as she was grateful to her in-laws, their assumption that they would make all decisions for her was wearing thin.

As was Lea's recent moodiness. To be fair, Lea wasn't as keen on the move to the coast as David was. Since he'd recovered from his serious illness a couple of years ago, Cathy had noticed that Lea was much more receptive to David's suggestions.

Now, most of her bossiness had moved to Cathy.

Maybe Lea had been the same with her boys?

Maybe that had something to do with Russ leaving. Cathy's thoughts circled in her head.

The journey into town was quiet, and not a word was spoken after they dropped off Billy and Josie.

'See you later. If I'm still in town, I'll pick you up at three. I'll park across the road, so look for the car before you get on the bus.'

'Can we go to the café for a milkshake if you are?' Josie asked.

'We can.'

As they turned off River Road, three white utilities were parked at the house—two small and one of those huge RAM ones; the site was a hive of activity. Timber and building supplies covered the front lawn and there was evidence of digging in the backyard. A lot of changes had been made since Cathy had been there two weeks earlier with the children.

She couldn't understand why Lea had wanted her input in the kitchen decision, because Lea had gotten her way with the stove.

It hadn't been worth the argument.

They parked on Court Street and Cathy locked the car door. Slipping her handbag over her shoulder, she followed Lea through the gate, along the front path and up the six timber stairs onto the porch.

The door was open and the smell of freshly-sawn timber and paint greeted them.

'Looks like Ryan's been working hard,' Lea said. 'He's achieved a lot since I was last here.'

Cathy looked around as she went into the

hall. 'It looks like a new house.'

'It does. I do hope you and the kids will be happy here, Cathy. I know you weren't happy about leaving the farm.'

'I'm fine about that, honestly, Lea. We need to give Jon and Cleo a fresh start in their life with their young family.'

Lea looked at her closely. 'And we need to get your life going again for you too.'

'I'm fine. I have a life with the kids. I want you and David to go down to the coast and not worry about us at all. *You* start having a life. You can't spend your time worrying about what's going on here. We're grown up now and we can look after ourselves.'

Lea stared at her, her face devoid of expression.

Russ was always the elephant in the room in every conversation.

'I'm going to look for a job in town, and the kids are really happy they can play Saturday sports now. And thanks to you and David, look at the lovely place we're going to live in.' Cathy spread her arms wide. She didn't mention to Lea that she fully intended to pay them rent once she had a job. That would be another argument, but she was determined to do it.

Ryan was beside the clothesline talking to

an unfamiliar man with short sandy coloured hair. The two of them looked up as Cathy and Lea walked out onto the small porch at the top of the back stairs.

'Careful where you walk, Ryan said. 'Joe's been digging holes around there ready for the new deck.'

'Hi, Cathy, hi, Lea,' Joe called up.

The smell of wet dirt met Cathy and she looked down to a couple of holes that Joe, Ryan's brother, had dug near the string line that ran across the width of the house. The holes were half full of water and the yard was a quagmire. 'We'll stay up here, I think,' she said.

'Hi, Joe, how are you?' Lea said.

'Good, thanks, Lea. A bit wet though,' he said wiping a muddy hand on his brow, leaving a streak of dirt.

'This rain has to stop soon,' Lea commented. 'We'll be into the summer storms before we know it. Not that I'll be here to see them.'

'You'll get them down on the coast,' Cathy said.

Ryan walked over to where they waited on the top step. The other man followed him over and Cathy frowned as she looked down at him. He looked familiar but she couldn't place him.

'Thanks for coming into town,' Ryan said. 'We'll come in the front way and you can meet Grant.'

Grant? The name didn't ring a bell.

By the time the two men left their muddy work boots on the front porch and walked down the hall in their socks, Lea and Cathy had discussed the benchtop arrangement.

'Cathy, Lea, this is Grant Cummings. He's the landscaper I've hired to do the work in the garden and to replace the fences.'

'Hello, Grant,' Lea said as Cathy tried to place him.

He nodded at them both. 'Good to meet you.'

'It's great to have you as project manager, Ryan. Saves us trying to find tradesmen. I know it's really hard in town at the moment,' Lea said.

'It is. I've got work lined up for about twelve months,' Ryan said. He glanced at Grant. 'I was telling Grant before you arrived that he'll have plenty of work in town.'

'You're new in town, are you, Grant?' Lea asked, and Cathy waited for his reply.

'Yes, I haven't been here long,' he said.

'How long do you think it will be before the work's finished, Ryan?' Cathy glanced at the landscape guy who was looking out the window at

49

the backyard.

'Have you decided on the benchtop?' Ryan looked from Lea to Cathy. 'A U-shape here or a straight bench? You could have a breakfast bar and some stools instead of filling up that small space with a kitchen table and chairs?'

'I said to Lea when we looked at it, I think the extended bench and the breakfast bar idea is good. The kids will each have a desk in their rooms for their homework.'

'Okay, it's only a matter of finishing off the cupboards, the last lick of paint in the kitchen and getting the floor down. I reckon we can do that in less than a week. I'll pull Joe off the yard, and we'll get inside finished for you. So if you're happy not to have the yard or the back deck done before you move in, you could come next weekend.'

'That's great,' Lea said. 'We can help Cathy move and then we go to the coast the weekend after that.'

Cathy turned to Grant. 'Will we be in your way if we move in while you're still working on the fence?'

He hesitated and his brow wrinkled in a quick frown before he shook his head. 'No, that will be fine.'

Even his voice was familiar, and Cathy tried to remember where she'd seen him before, but couldn't think. She must have stared too long because Grant raised his eyebrows as she stared at him.

'Was there something else you needed?' he asked. There was no recognition in his expression. She must have him mixed up with someone else.

'No, all good.' She forced a smile. He certainly didn't have Ryan's charm. The next time she saw Jaclyn, she'd asked where Grant was from.

'Grant's started a landscaping business down near the nursery.'

'So, you're here to stay, Grant?' Lea asked.

'For the time being.'

Cathy didn't know what Grant Cumming's problem was, but he seemed very closed down. She knew that she could be hard to engage, but she was always self-conscious about being abandoned by Russ Kendall, the son of a long-standing Bindarra Creek family.

If Grant was going to be working in the yard, she'd keep the door shut and stay out of his way after they moved in.

Maybe she could say to Lea that they didn't need the place landscaped. He could build the fences and leave.

Cathy held back a sigh. Lea knew what she wanted to be done, and it was her house, so Cathy knew she would just have to put up with him.

Chapter 6

Saturday dawned bright and clear; the rain of the past few weeks seemed to have cleared away, despite the continuous warnings on the media of the likelihood of storms and flash flood.

'I sometimes think, they like to keep us scared,' Cathy commented to Cleo as she carried a box of toys into the living room.

Cleo wrinkled her nose. 'Who?'

Cathy laughed. 'Sorry, I was just thinking about the weather forecasters. All doom and gloom. They said there was a seventy percent chance of rain today and look out there. Not a cloud in the sky.'

'It's only early, although I agree the media hypes it up. Like everything else these days.'

'I suppose it is early. Cleo, there's a heap of toys here that the kids have outgrown. If you don't want them, just leave them in the box and I'll take them to the op shop next week.'

'Thanks.' Cleo pushed herself out of the chair and put both hands on her lower back.

'You okay?'

'Yes, just the early cramps. I'm fine, but I'll be glad when the baby's born. Cathy? Can I ask you

52

something?'

Cathy put the box on the coffee table. 'Sure, what's up.'

Cleo bit her lip. 'I feel bad that you and the kids are moving out. It's all been such a rush. I suggested to Lea that you might like to stay, but she wouldn't have a bar of it.'

'It's fine. We're all really looking forward to moving into town.'

'Honestly? You're not just saying that?'

'Honestly.' Cathy glanced out the window. David and Lea had just left with the truckload of her stuff, and she was going to drive into town shortly, so she knew she could speak without fear of being overheard.

'I'm probably speaking out of turn here, but I think David insisted on their move to the coast for some solid reasons. With him being sick a couple of years ago, he knows he can't look after the place like he used to, and I think if Lea had had her way, they would have expected you and Jon to move in here with them. I love Lea, but she can be hard to live with.'

'I know, Cathy. I was always scared they would expect that, but I worry about you with the way things have turned out.'

'Don't you worry one bit. It's worked out well. Living in town is going to be good for all of us.' The more Cathy told herself that, the more she was starting to believe it. 'Anyway, I have to grab the kids and go in now. If Lea unpacks the boxes, I'll never find anything.'

'You're right about that. She's even arranged my cupboards since we've been here.' Cathy chuckled. 'But she means well. We'll come in and visit once you're settled. I go in and see Gran every week.'

'I forgot Esther was your grandma. I'd love a visit every week. Very much.' Cathy leaned over and hugged Cleo. 'Thanks for being a great sister-in-law. I still think back to high school when I was part of that group who were so mean to you and Chrissie and Janice.'

'We were all at that teenage bitchiness age then, although I must admit I'm always quite cold to Nina when I see her in town.'

'She was a nasty type. I stay well away from them all these days,' Cathy said. 'Anyway, they all dropped me when I fell pregnant with Billy. It was cool to have sex, but very uncool to get pregnant. Nina always told everyone I did it deliberately to trap Russ.'

'She's always been a cow. Jon hired her brother, Mike, for shearing a few years back, but he didn't work out. He's a bit light-fingered apparently.'

'I haven't seen him for ten years. He was mates with Russ at high school. Last I heard he was in jail.'

'We worry about you, Cathy. Not knowing what happened to Russ must be so hard. Jon was talking about it last night. I admire you for how strong you are, and what a wonderful mother you are to Billy and Josie. I just hope I can be as good with our kids.'

Cathy didn't want to hear what they'd been talking about. Her voice was brisk. 'Of course you're a great mum. Look at you now with little Benny. And sweetie, don't you worry about me. I've had ten years to get over it and move on, and now that I'll be more independent, it will be even easier. I'll see you soon.'

She hurried out to the backyard without looking back at Cleo. 'Come on, you pair. It's time to go,' she called to Billy and Josie.

Both of the kids were already waiting at the car. 'Wow, you must be keen to go,' Cathy said. 'Nan and Pa have taken the truck in, and we have to hurry up to get to town.'

'I said goodbye to all the girls,' Josie said. 'And I told Uncle Jon how much to feed them. He said he'd bring the eggs into town to us.'

'Once we get settled, we'll get our own chooks from the produce store. I promise,' Cathy said as she waited for the kids to get into the back seat. 'And thank you, you've both been a really good help today.'

'We're really excited about moving,' Billy said. 'It's going to be so good.'

'It will be. Once the yard is fenced and it's all ours, we can settle in.'

Cathy started the car and as they drove down the drive to the gate, she looked back at the farm where they'd spent the last ten years. Josie had known no other home, and Billy wouldn't remember living at River Cottage.

Cathy did, and even though she was happy to be leaving the farm, she still wasn't sure how she felt about moving back to the home she had lived in with Russ.

She took a deep breath and told herself that it would be good. They would make the best of it.

A whole new chapter of their lives was about to begin.

***

Grant had spent the rest of the week working in the backyard of River Cottage. To his great relief, Joe and Ryan had worked inside, quickly finishing off the work that needed to be done. When they decided to work on Saturday to give the kitchen the final coat of paint, he said he'd come across to the house too.

He'd measured up for the fence and ordered the Colourbond panels from Tamworth yesterday, and today he was marking out the areas for a couple of garden boxes. The sides and front yard of the house were going to remain lawn for the time being. He hadn't been back to the house at night. It would be too obvious if he dug around where Joe was working. That would have to wait.

'We'll leave it up to Cathy,' Ryan said this morning when Grant had asked about the front yard. 'Focus on the back. The fence and the gardens, and I think we'll demolish the chook shed and build a new one. Young Josie's right into her chooks.'

'Josie?' Grant frowned.

Ryan paused before he went to the front porch. 'Cathy has two kids. Billy's just started high school, and Josie's about ten.'

'Ah, I didn't know that,' Grant said. 'Not that it matters.'

But it did, it mattered so much. He hadn't done his homework properly. Slip up on one thing, and others would follow.

Sally had called last night to see if he'd found anything yet.

'No, I've been working, and I haven't had a chance. How's Beau?'

'The same,' his sister said with a sigh. 'I was called up to the school again yesterday. One more suspension and they're going to expel him, the deputy said. He's in with a bad group, and I can't even keep him at home. He just walks out on me. When this money comes through, we're going to move. A whole new start.'

Grant didn't like to say it, but Sally and Beau had had several new starts. He'd funded a move to Armidale, and then a move down to Newcastle, but Sally always came home broke and with Beau even more unsettled.

'If he does get expelled, could he go over to Bindarra Creek and work as a labourer for you? It would get him away from those boys.'

'I'll think about it.'

'Please, Grant. You of all people know what it's like to get sucked into a group like that.'

Ignoring his sister's dig, Grant's voice was short. 'I'll talk to you later in the week when I get a chance to look around River Cottage. I really think Mike's full of it. If there was anything buried there, he would have done something about it years ago.'

'He's not been able to. He's been in jail.'

'What! And you've been to see him? God, Sally, you make some poor choices.'

'No, we've been writing to each other. He asked me in a letter a few months ago, before I mentioned it to you.'

'Then that makes it doubly suss. I knew it would be if Mike was involved, but you didn't ever tell me he was in jail. Not that I'm a bit surprised to hear that,' he said, bitterness lacing his tone.

'I want you to still look. I told Mike that someone was moving into the cottage, and he freaked. He wants it found before someone else does. He said he'll give me half because of Russ.'

'Russ Kendall's not around anymore. Look, Sally, I don't like the sound of this. If there's something in that backyard, maybe we should let the police know and they can sort it out.'

'No. I want my share. I deserve it.' Her tone was shrill.

'I'll think about it,' he said.

'Keep in touch, please. I appreciate what you do for us. I do love you, you know. You are the best big brother a girl could have, Gee.'

He knew Sally was trying to soften him up using his nickname, but that made him crankier. That was what everyone had called him in Bindarra Creek, and he'd made sure he'd stayed with Grant when he moved on.

Grant had worked carefully around the yard through the week, aware that Ryan and Joe could see what he was doing if they looked outside, so he resisted the temptation to poke around. He'd have to come back one night after the footings for the deck had been poured and cover his tracks. He knew exactly where to dig, but it was too close to where Joe was working. Any disturbance in the ground would be obvious. He had no reason to be digging a hole where the edge of the deck was going to be. There was no fence or gardens going anywhere near there.

Most of his thoughts had been taken up this week with the knowledge that Cathy Kendall had kids. Why hadn't he known that? He wondered if Sally knew, but he wasn't going to ask until he had things sorted at this end.

He'd been kidding himself for three months that what he was about to do was being done for a good reason, but knowing now that Russ Kendall had fathered two children with Cathy, had put a totally different perspective on everything. He'd even dreamed about the lot of them last night.

'Bloody hell,' Grant muttered as he swung the mattock on Friday afternoon, cleaning the bush away from the corner where the chook pen would go.

'What's up, Grant? You don't sound very happy.'

Grant jumped and dropped the mattock as Ryan's voice came from beside him. He'd been so lost in his thoughts he hadn't heard Ryan approach.

Grant forced a grin to his face. 'Nothing bad. I was just thinking about my tax.'

'Your tax?'

'Yeah, with the move and getting myself sorted I just remembered I forgot to do my BAS at the end of September. I'll probably get fined.'

It wasn't a lie, either. He'd been so caught up in the move and this Bindarra Creek shit, he had forgotten to do his BAS.

Ryan shook his head. 'Mate, I'm a builder and a manager. That's why I've handed it over. I can hook you up with a good accountant in town if you want. Rowan Harris. His wife, Chrissie grew up here and they've made the "country change". He's doing a good job with my stuff. I used to do it all myself, but Jaclyn sat me down and made me see sense. "You're a builder," she said. "And you're running a business and you need to delegate." Best thing I ever did.' Ryan's smile was curious. 'You're not married, mate?'

'Nuh. Not for me. I move around too much. And I've never met anyone I thought I could live with.' Grant's tension eased and he bent down to pick up the dirt-encrusted mattock. That was all truthful.

He hated this deception. It would be good to just come out and say. 'Look mate, why I'm here is—'

'Hello?'

Ryan and Grant turned together. A truck was backing down the side of the house. Lea was waving to them.

Ryan grinned. 'How about we meet for a beer at the Riverside Pub when we knock off today, and we can finish our chat? It's Saturday, and we've had a big week.'

Grant nodded as Ryan walked across to the truck. 'Sounds good to me.' He had a lot of time for Ryan and Joe, and they hadn't lived here when he had, so there would be no awkward questions. He'd just have to be careful who else he talked to at the pub.

'Great timing, Dave,' Ryan called out. 'Joe's just cleaning up in the kitchen and we're done. We'll give you a hand to unpack the truck. Grant, are you done now? Give us a hand?'

Grant waved an acknowledgment. 'I'll just pack up my gear.'

As he walked back towards the truck after putting the spade and mattock on the back of his ute, an older guy climbed slowly out of the truck.

'Grant, this is Dave Kendall. Dave, Grant Cummings, new to town.'

Grant froze as Dave looked at him quizzically. 'Cummings?'

'Yeah.' Grant swallowed the nervous

tension that recognition brought, forcing himself to relax.

'Greg Cummings' son?'

'Greg's my dad.' He forced a casual grin to his face. 'Did you know him? We lived in town for a few years when I was at high school. He and Mum are in Melbourne now.'

'You used to hang around with our son and his mates.'

'Your son?'

'Russell Kendall.'

It was all Grant could do not to react. He frowned and shook his head slightly. 'Not that I remember. I wasn't at the high school long.'

'Must have you mixed up with someone else. There was a big crowd of them back in those days.' Dave stared at him for a while and then shrugged before he turned back to the truck. 'Most of them were bloody troublemakers.'

Ryan waited at the back of the small truck until Dave had gone into the house with Lea. 'Don't mind Dave, mate. They had a bit of a family tragedy, and he can be pretty sullen. Jac and I both think that's why they're so keen to move away. It's been ten years.'

'Tragedy?' Grant asked quietly.

'Russ was Cathy's husband. He went missing. Disappeared one night and was never seen again. Credit cards and phone weren't touched, so the consensus is that he's dead. Maybe drowned in the Akuna River.'

'Sad. Kids too, you said the other day?'

'Yep, it was before we moved here, but apparently, Cathy had just had Josie. They lived here at the cottage, so the river theory was pretty strong, I heard. You can't believe what's said, but the word was he was drinking over at the caravan park across the road with some mates and took a wrong turn on the way home.'

'Nope, you can't believe gossip, can you? In a situation like that everyone has their theories.'

Ryan looked at him curiously. 'You didn't know Russ?'

Grant's heart skittered and the lie put a bad taste in his mouth. 'The name's familiar, but I was pretty quiet at school. One of those boring students who put their head down and did my work.'

Ryan chuckled. 'You must meet Jaclyn. She'll love you for that. She had some doozies of students when she first came here. The previous boss had let the school run wild.'

Grant grinned, forcing himself to stay calm. 'I'd guess that was the same headmaster that was there when I was there. He was a shocker. Old Kev, we used to call him. He'd been there for years, and they reckoned they were going to have to carry him out in a box when he carked it. God, kids can be cruel, can't they?'

'I'm sure that was the name Jac mentioned. But he lived to tell the tales. Apparently, he won the lottery and moved to a flash house in Sydney. Come on, we'll help them unload and then go for a beer.'

Good, thought Grant. He and Russ had spent many an afternoon in Stricko's office. At least he wouldn't be there to tell the tales Grant didn't want told.

Chapter 7

Cathy had just turned onto Main Street when a raucous squawking came from the back of the car. She glanced into the rear vision mirror and caught Josie's eye.

'Oh, Josie, you didn't, did you?'

Billy giggled. 'She did. I told her not to.'

'You did not, Billy Kendall!' Josie squealed.

'Did so!'

'Stop it, you pair.' Cathy was hard-pressed to keep the smile off her face. 'Josie, please tell me that's not Red setting up that racket in the boot.'

'He's in a box, Mummy. I had to bring him. When I went to say goodbye, he looked really upset. It's bad enough that the girls will miss me, but they have each other and Red had no one.'

'And pray tell, how does a rooster look upset?'

Billy snorted.

'He just did. His feathers were all fluffed up,' Josie said. 'I know him better than anyone. And there's a chook shed there for him, so he won't be a nuisance.'

'But no decent fences, sweetheart. If he gets run over—'

Billy snorted again. 'If he gets run over,

we'll have roast chicken for tea.'

Josie curled up her fist and leaned across to hit her brother.

'Stop right there, young lady.' Cathy eased off on the accelerator as they approached River Cottage. If you hit your brother, I'll turn the car around right now and take Red home.'

'This is his home,' Josie muttered. 'His new home.'

'And it's our new home, and the same rules apply as they did at Nan and Pa's. You two will speak nicely to each other, show your manners and no fighting. Okay?'

Silence from the back seat.

'Billy?'

'Yes, Mum. Good manners, no fighting.'

'Josie?' Cathy glanced in the rear vision mirror again to see her daughter's bottom lip out and her arms folded. 'Josie,' she repeated, a warning tone in her voice.

'Yes, Mummy. I'll be good. As long as Billy is good to me.'

'Good, that's all sorted then. And don't take off. You can each carry a box from the boot and help unpack it in the house.'

'Then can I go and look at the river?' Billy asked.

'We'll see later. I'll walk over with you the

first time.' Cathy turned the motor off and popped the boot, forgetting about the rooster in there.

'Mummy,' Josie squealed again, pushing her door open and jumping out. 'Red might escape.'

By the time Cathy got around to the back of the car, Josie had the box with the rooster secure under her arm.

'Billy, you go into the backyard with Josie and see if you can lock that bird in the shed. Then you can both come back and help unload the car and the truck.' Cathy wagged a finger. 'And don't get your shoes muddy.'

Cathy took her handbag out of the car along with the small esky with food in it. Just enough for the weekend; she intended to fill the pantry on Monday after she had coffee with Jaclyn. She glanced in the back of the truck as she walked along the driveway to see what was left there and was surprised to see it was almost empty.

Cathy had insisted on leaving Lea's furniture at the farm, and she'd dipped into her meagre saving to buy three new beds and a second-hand fridge for River Cottage. She would go to Dodge and Tessa's shop next week and see what she could pick up in the way of tables and chairs, and maybe a sofa. Jaclyn had suggested garage sales in Tamworth too and had offered to go over with her. Cathy planned to go there next week to pick up some crockery and appliances for the kitchen from Big W.

Everything that she'd had when she and Russ had lived here before was old and needed replacing. She'd taken some linen at Lea's insistence, as her linen press was full.

Then she needed to find a job.

Voices drifted through the open window as she walked along the side of the house to the front steps. As she listened to the laughter in there, she picked up Grant's laugh straight away, and she stopped walking. She knew that laugh.

And suddenly it struck Cathy. She remembered who Grant was.

Gee Cummings.

He was much taller and broader, and his long blonde hair had gone and was slightly darker now, but she was sure it was him.

Russ had called him Gee when they were at school, although she only remembered him when Russ was in Year 11. The year she had first fallen for Russ. It was cool in those days to hang with the bad guys. Nina Potter had left her alone for a few months until Russ had dropped Cathy and moved on to the next girl.

Sally Cummings. She'd been in Russ's year, and she'd left town soon after. She wondered if Sally was a relation to Grant, but he'd already left school and moved away by then, so maybe not.

Biting her lip thoughtfully as she walked up the front steps, Cathy wondered if Grant had recognised her. He'd shown no sign of it the other day. Strange that he hadn't mentioned it. He'd only been on the fringes of the large group that sat together at lunchtime behind A block where they could smoke unseen, but she knew that he'd hung around with Russ and Mike Potter after school. He'd always been polite to her—on the few occasions he'd spoken to her—but as far as she could remember he hadn't come back to Year 12 after the Christmas holidays.

Cathy followed the voices down the hall and when she walked into the kitchen, Lea had boiled the kettle and was pouring out tea.

Stupidly, a shaft of resentment pierced Cathy; this was supposed to be their home, but Lea, as usual, was making her mark.

Cathy chastised herself, thinking how stupid and unfair she was being; they were all here to help her.

Moving back to River Cottage was bothering her more than she'd thought it would.

His presence in her memories was so strong, she'd half expected to see Russ walking down the hall behind her.

'Hi, everyone,' she said quietly.

'Cup of tea, Cath?' Lea asked.

'Yes, please. It's been a big morning, hasn't it?' She looked around the kitchen. 'This is beautiful, thank you, Ryan. And you too, Joe. I'm looking forward to cooking here.'

'On your new stove,' Lea said.

'Yes, on my new stove.'

She glanced at Grant. 'I see the new fence panels have been delivered, Grant. You're working fast too. Thank you.'

He nodded. 'It won't take long.' As he looked away and down at his mug, Cathy examined him more closely. If it hadn't been for hearing his laugh, she doubted if she would have recognised him. It must have been twelve or thirteen years since she'd last seen him. Grant Cummings had grown into a fine-looking man. Strong-featured and clear-eyed, if he smiled more often, he'd be a real looker. For the first time in a long time, her tummy fluttered with female appreciation as she watched him.

Each time she'd seen him, his clothes had been pressed and clean, and he looked as though he took pride in how he looked. Out of the three utes parked outside, she'd noticed Grant's was always clean, and the equipment on the back was always arranged tidily. As much as Ryan and Joe were good workers, their utes were always muddy and loaded with a variety of farm equipment as well as their building tools.

Grant Coleman had class.

She nodded slowly and then her cheeks heated as she realised that he was looking back at her curiously—and with a hint of challenge—in his eyes.

Maybe he'd picked up that she'd twigged who he was, but she wasn't going to say a word, especially in front of Lea and David, or it would turn into yet another conversation about Russ.

She was the first to look away as Lea held out a mug of tea.

'Thanks, Lea.'

'Where're the kids?' Lea asked. 'Gone exploring already? You watch them at that river.'

'I've already told them they're not to go over there without me.' Cathy shook her head. 'I told them to come in here and help. They've gone to put Red in the chook shed. Josie smuggled him into the boot.'

David burst out laughing and it made Cathy smile. 'That's our Josie,' he said.

'The chook shed?' When she turned to him, Grant was frowning as he looked at Ryan.

'Uh oh,' Joe said.

'What's wrong? Isn't it secure?' Cathy asked.

'It sort of is, but it was about to be dismantled this afternoon.'

'Oh dear,' she said. 'David, maybe you'll have to take Red home in the truck.'

Grant walked over to the sink and rinsed his cup. 'I'm sure we can put together something temporary while we demolish and rebuild the shed.'

'Or we can build the new one closer to the deck, and demolish the old one when we're finished,' Ryan said.

Grant's expression seemed strangely relieved. 'An excellent idea. Leave it with me and I'll have a poke around out there this afternoon.'

Cath's voice trembled. 'You are all being so kind to us. I really appreciate it.'

Gant caught her eye and for the first time, he really smiled. 'Our pleasure. It's my first job in Bindarra Creek and I have to make a good impression. I'm sure you have lots of friends who might be looking for a landscaper.'

Cathy chuckled. 'Not really, but if anyone asks, I'm sure I can pass your name along.'

'Don't tell Jac, will you, Cathy? She's been on at me to build a new garden out the front for months.'

'And then it's about time you did, young man,' Lea said. 'Don't you know wives' requests come first? Isn't that right, Grant?' She was

73

obviously digging.

Grant put his hands up. 'As a confirmed bachelor, I can't answer that question.'

'And on that note, we'll head out and get back to work, and suss out this chook shed,' Ryan said. 'Come on, Joe.'

'Thanks for your help,' David said. 'Lea, it's time we got going too. Jon wants me to help him drench some cattle this afternoon.'

As Cathy followed them outside, Josie and Billy came around the side, each carrying a small box. She smiled as they both carefully wiped their boots on the mat on the front porch.

Contentment stole over Cathy. Everything was going to be all right. She put her arms around her children's shoulders, and they all waved to Lea and David as the truck pulled out of the driveway.

Chapter 8

Once she got used to the creaks and groans of the old house as it settled for the night, Cathy began to relax. The cottage wasn't used to having people inside, as much as she wasn't used to being in a different house.

Billy and Josie had gone to bed early, excited and worn out from running around the back garden dodging the holes Joe had dug and then settling Red for the night.

Cathy wondered what time he'd start crowing in the morning. The chook enclosure was a hundred metres from the house out at the farm and about ten metres away from the cottage. She had a feeling they'd all be up early tomorrow.

No matter, there was plenty to do. Their clothes were still in boxes, along with assorted toys and books, and personal possessions that had to be put away. Ryan had installed new built-in wardrobes in each of the three bedrooms.

Just after dinner, Billy had come in with an earnest look on his face and she knew she was about to be hit up for something when he snuggled in for a cuddle. Even though she knew he was after something, she still enjoyed the comfort of her son's rare cuddle. Clean PJs, a fresh fragrance of soap and toothpaste came from one very clean almost teenager. She wondered how much longer she'd get cuddles; they were becoming more infrequent as he grew up.

'Mum?'

'Yes, Billy?' She smoothed his damp hair back as he looked up at her.

'Do you think we could have our own dog here?'

'That doesn't sound like such a bad idea.'

His grin spread wide.

'Let's get settled in first, mate, and then maybe we'll go look when we know we'll stay here for sure.'

'Where else would we go?' he asked indignantly, as though a ridiculous statement had been made.

'Just be patient, Billy. We'll talk about it in a few weeks. We've still got no fence and the yard's not big enough for a dog pen, and we couldn't tie one up. It would be cruel.'

'It could live inside,' he ventured.

'Nope. We live inside. Dogs live outside.'

'It's not fair. Josie's got her rooster, and I left the dogs out at Pa and Nan's farm.'

'Billy.' Cathy's tone held a warning note. She tried to be patient, but she was tired from the move. Not just today—that had been quite pleasant. Trying to sort out ten years of stuff and remember what was hers and what she should leave behind had been hard.

Not that it really mattered if she left anything behind; this move was a fresh start. When she had a job and could afford luxuries, she was going to turn River Cottage into a little home for them. Already, the memories of living here with Russ were fading. The house was so different now, the harsh memories that had been made here weren't coming as frequently as she'd expected.

She looked down at her wrist and remembered the night in this room when Russ had pinned her to the wall with her hands above her head. Her wrist had been purple for a fortnight and had been so sore, she'd had to peg the nappies on the line one-handed. There had been a mark on the wall where the plaster had been chipped by her trying to get away, but it had been fixed and painted over in the renovation.

At least the bed was new; there were no memories there either.

She left Billy's room, and went into Josie's, bent down and brushed her lips over warm sweet-smelling cheeks and padded barefoot down the hall. Making a cup of tea, she sat in their sole bean bag on the floor in the living room and enjoyed the silence.

David had insisted on buying a huge smart television for the kids, and as Cathy turned it off, she knew moving into town had been the right choice. Maybe not to River Cottage with its memories, but it was satisfying sitting here by herself, not having to have the television on, and if she chose to watch something, having control of the remote.

Being in a house by themselves, they could decide what was for dinner, and what time the children should go to bed. She relished the freedom of her own decision-making and realised how much Lea and David had guided their everyday lives.

As much as she loved them, Lea and David were the in-laws of a long-dead relationship.

A relationship that had been dead long before Russ had left them; if she really thought about it, there had rarely been a happy day in the two years they were together. When David found out Cathy was pregnant, he'd tried to get Russ to marry her. But a pregnant eighteen-year-old was not what Russ wanted. To his credit, he had moved into River Cottage with her when his parents had offered it, but there'd been no money, no job or possessions, and certainly no love.

Not that she would ever tell him, but Billy was the result of a one-night mistake after a few too many drinks after the football grand final. After paying no attention to her since she'd idolised him in Year 8, Russ had pursued her for a few weeks, and she had ignored him because he'd shown his true colours by then. And that was like a red rag to a bull to twenty-three-year-old Russ.

Cathy had been pregnant when she had sat her final school exams and her dreams of going to university had disappeared.

Her parents had disowned her, and Aunty Jean had told her when they had passed away within a year of each other. Her experience with her parents had made her more determined to be the best mother she possibly could. Her children came first.

Always.

She realised now she should have left the farm much earlier, but the pressure from Lea to stay so they could "make amends" as she called it had kept Cathy there.

Plus, the knowledge that they had lost their older son and she didn't want to add to that by taking their two grandchildren away from them.

They were here now, and she had no regrets. There were so many positives:

She had two beautiful children.

Russ was gone for good.

They had a lovely cottage to live in, and

there was a chance of a job at the school.

She was beginning to make friends, and the reaction that she'd had to Grant Cummings today had reassured her she was still had womanly feelings.

Today was a new beginning. The beginning of the rest of their lives.

A small smile crept over Cathy's face as she dozed in the bean bag. Next week, she'd have a comfy sofa to sit on

Half an hour later she rinsed her cup and turned it upside down on the sink. She'd refused the dishwasher that Lea had attempted to buy. She took a shower in the small bathroom that David had insisted on being re-tiled, made her way to the front bedroom and snuggled into the soft mattress.

Cathy had just started to drift off to sleep when a shrill scream had her rigid in the bed. She jumped out and raced up the hall to the kids' bedrooms.

Josie's bedroom door was open and from the door, Cathy could see her bed was empty.

Billy stumbled out of his room rubbing his eyes. 'What was that noise, Mum?'

'I don't know,' Cathy said. 'Is Josie in your room?'

'No, she should be in bed.'

Quickly checking the toilet and the rest of

the house, it was soon obvious Josie wasn't inside.

'Quick, come with me. We'll go out the front way because the back steps aren't safe.'

As Cathy flung open the front door, Josie came running around the side of the house. 'Mummy, Mummy, help. Quick, Mummy, save me.'

'Josie! Sweetheart. What are you doing out here? What's wrong?'

'The man, Mummy. Make the man go away.'

Cathy pulled her close and led her inside and locked the door behind them. 'What man, Josie? Tell me how you got outside.'

A dozen worst-case scenarios of kidnapping, abduction and worse flitted through Cathy's mind like a sped-up movie reel.

'Red was upset. I heard Red. He was kicking up a stink, Mummy, so I went out the back door. There was a man . . . a man . . . a real scary man in the backyard, and he tried to grab me and I screamed. He was in the backyard and I ran away from him.'

Her little body was trembling, and perspiration dotted her brow. Cathy led her daughter into her bedroom. 'Billy, go and get a glass of water for Josie, and get the face washer out of the shower and wet it and bring it here, please.'

Cathy held Josie tightly and tried to calm her shivering. 'It's okay, baby. I've got you. I won't let anyone hurt you.' She would kill anyone who tried to harm her two children. Kill them without a second thought.

'You're wet? How did you get wet?'

Billy came back in with a glass of water and put it on the floor beside the bed, and then handed the face washer to Cathy.

'Do you want me to go outside and check around, Mum?' he asked.

Cathy's heart turned over with love for her boy. 'No, Billy. We'll stay inside. Can you get my phone off the kitchen bench please?'

She'd call the police, although the chances of anyone being there were probably zero. There was no point calling Jon or Dave; it would take them half an hour to get into town, and she didn't know anyone else in town well enough to call for help. Ryan and Jaclyn were half an hour in the other direction.

Cathy could have wept, she felt so alone and helpless.

She wiped Josie's face gently and gradually her daughter's trembling eased. She wiped the mud off her little girl's arms and gently washed her feet.

'I fell in a hole, Mummy. I fell in one of those holes Joe dug.'

'We're going to get you a clean T-shirt'—Cathy gestured to Billy with her head, and he hurried out to Josie's room— 'and then we're all going to sleep in my bed. Are you okay now, sweetie?'

'I'm better now. That man with the shiny head has gone. I think he ran up the road. He won't come back, will he?'

'Shiny head? What do you mean a shiny head?'

Before Josie could answer, someone pounded on the front door. Cathy yelled, 'Billy, quick, come back to my room.'

The knocking came again but this time it was followed by a voice. 'Cathy, it's me, Grant. Grant Cummings. Are you all okay in there?'

Grant? What was he doing out there at this time of night? Was he the man Josie had seen in the backyard? She didn't know anything about Grant these days, and she sure wasn't going to trust him. Why on earth would he be here knocking on her door?

Billy scurried back in carrying a T-shirt for Josie and his eyes were wide. 'Will I let Mr Cummings in?'

'No. You stay here with Josie. I'll go and talk to him.'

'Be careful, Mummy.' Billy's voice shook.

'I will, sweetheart. Close the bedroom door behind me and lock it.'

Her hands trembled as she walked to the front door in her nightie. Billy did as he was told, and Cathy could hear Josie crying again.

She went to the front door and pressed her hands against it. 'Grant?'

'Cathy? Are you all okay?'

'Why?'

I was driving past and I saw Josie running like the wind, and I could hear her screaming.'

'Why were you driving past at this time of night?'

'I've been out with Ryan and Joe. We ended up staying at the pub for dinner and making a night of it. Cathy, are you all right?'

Cathy hesitated, unsure whether to believe him or not. 'Stay there. I'll be back in a minute.'

She hurried down to the kitchen and got her phone from the bench. She glanced at the time; it was only just after nine-thirty.

She pressed the speed dial for Jaclyn, and waited until it picked up.

'Cathy?' Jaclyn sounded as though she'd been asleep.

'Jac, yes, it's me. This might sound silly, but did Ryan go out with Joe and Grant tonight?'

'Yes, he did, why?' Jaclyn's voice held a

note of panic. 'Is Ryan all right? There hasn't been an accident, has there?'

'No, sorry I just needed to check. I'll tell you why later.'

'Ryan rang me about ten minutes ago to let me know he was on the way home.'

'Thanks. That's all I needed to know. Sorry to bother you. I'll call in the morning.'

Cathy put the phone on the bed and walked slowly back to the front door. 'Are you still there?'

'I am.'

She reached up and unlocked the deadlock and then turned the door handle, hoping she wasn't making a huge mistake. But she needed someone else here to support her. As Cathy pulled the door open, her hands were shaking like Josie's had been.

So much for her newfound independence.

Grant stepped forward but stayed in the doorway. 'Tell me what happened, Cathy.'

'I was asleep and Josie's screams woke me up. I went to her room and she wasn't there or inside anywhere. When I opened this door, she came up the steps screaming and I brought her inside.'

'Is she hurt? Is she all right?'

'She's just upset and scared.' Cathy stared at him. 'What did you see? Why did you come to the door?'

'I saw Josie running around the side. Your front security light came on. You grabbed her and took her inside and shut the door.'

'Why did it take you so long to come and knock on the door?'

'Because . . .'

'Because why?' Cathy clasped her hands to her chest and then realised she was only wearing her short white nightie.

'Because I saw someone come out through the old fence. From your backyard. I almost ran him over.'

'Who was it?'

Grant ran his hand through his hair. 'Look, I don't know many people in town. All I can tell you is, he was a big guy, had a sizable beer gut and a bald head. He took off down towards the river.'

'A bald shiny head?'

'Yes, I guess you could describe it like that. Why?'

'That's what Josie said. "A man with a shiny head," so I guess that counts you out, Grant. I'm sorry I was suspicious. I was about to call the police when you knocked on the door.'

'That's fine. I'm not precious. I was worried that something had happened when I heard Josie screaming.' Grant looked over her head and she could see his mind ticking over. 'Did you hear anyone trying to get into the house?'

'I don't think so, but I was asleep.'

'Why was Josie outside anyway?'

'She said she heard the rooster setting up a fuss. Knowing her she would have gone out to bring Red into the laundry. They're used to being out on the farm and neither of the kids has any fear of the dark or being outside at night. They're country kids; that's all they've ever known. I'm going to have to teach them some town sense. Especially with that caravan park across the road. I think it might be a bit dodgy. Do you think he might have come from over there?'

'I don't know, but I'll follow it up in the morning. I'll recognise him if I see him. Is Josie okay now?'

Cathy put her hand to her mouth. 'I should be in there with them.'

'Where are they?'

'In my room. I told Billy to lock the bedroom door while I came to see what you wanted.' She looked up at him and his eyes held hers. An unfamiliar rippling warmth headed south, and heat filled her cheeks. 'Thank you, Grant. I appreciate you coming to check on us. I'm sorry I doubted you.'

His voice was gruff. 'You were sensible. You don't know me. Go and check on the kids and then I'll go. There's probably no point calling the police now. They'll be closed.'

'Yes, you're right. It'll go through to Tamworth. I'll wait until tomorrow.'

Cathy walked down the hall, conscious of Grant standing near the front door, and very aware of her short nightie and bare legs. Billy was holding Josie and her eyelids were drooping. 'Hop into bed and make room for me. I'll be back when—' she'd been about to say when I check all the doors and windows, but she didn't want to frighten Josie— 'when I say goodbye to Mr Cummings.'

'It was good of him to check on us, Mum,' Billy said.

'It was. Now snuggle up. I'll be back in a moment.'

Grant was still waiting by the front door.

'They're fine,' she said. 'Almost asleep.'

She was taken aback when Grant reached out and took her hand.

'What about you, Cathy? You're still trembling. Are you going to be okay here tonight? Would you like me to camp outside in my ute?'

She shook her head. 'Thank you, I appreciate it, but we'll be fine.'

'Where's your phone?'

'In the kitchen.'

He pulled his phone out of his shirt pocket.

'What's your number? I'll text you and then you'll have my number. Call me at any time through the night if you need to.'

She reeled her number off and watched his hands as he typed it into his phone. His hands were tanned with a light sprinkling of fine hair and his fingernails were clipped and clean.

He looked up and held her eyes again. 'Promise you'll call if you're at all worried. Whatever time it is.'

'I promise. I will. Thank you, Grant.'

Cathy locked the door and leaned her back against it as she listened to his footsteps going down the front stairs. Her phone dinged as his message came in.

What had happened to her there? One kind gesture from a good-looking man, and she hadn't been able to take her eyes off him.

Chapter 9

Grant didn't head straight home. He knew exactly who he was looking for, and he wanted to see him before Cathy went to the police tomorrow.

The last thing he wanted was his name brought up in an investigation.

What the hell had Mike Potter been doing in the backyard tonight? He was supposed to be in jail. Mick had written Sally about what he'd maintained was buried there, and all she could think of was the chance of getting money. Grant had never believed Russ when he'd told him what he and Mike Potter were going to do, and insist he help them. He'd thought it was yet another instance of Russ Kendall big-noting himself.

Maybe not.

Grant had been determined to prove it untrue once and for all and get Sally off his back. All she could ever see was the money. A chance of easy money. He wondered now with Mick Potter hanging around whether it was actually true. He certainly didn't like the idea of him being in Cathy's yard.

For a brief moment, he considered telling Cathy who he was and what he was looking for but immediately thought better of it. He wondered how much she knew. Maybe she knew about the money too.

As Grant drove around the block and then approached the caravan park from the other side, he tried to analyse why he was so worried about Cathy. He hadn't been completely honest with her concerning the night's events.

Not only had he almost run Mike Potter over, but he'd turned his headlights off, pulled over, and watched where he'd gone.

He went into the caravan park, and Grant watched him go to a small permanent dwelling facing the road about a hundred metres away from River Cottage.

He didn't trust Mike at all, and the thought that he was so close to Cathy's cottage and might go back there worried him.

Grant pulled up and sat in the ute after he switched the lights off. How had he let Cathy get under his skin so quickly?

She had an air of gentle vulnerability around her, but Grant had been around long enough to know that that was often a ruse to keep a man interested. He'd watched his sister do it many times.

It didn't help that Cathy was a very attractive woman. Her olive skin and cat-shaped green eyes gave her an exotic appearance; not that she did anything to enhance her attraction. Her dark hair was always pulled back into a simple ponytail, and until tonight, he'd only ever seen her in jeans and T-shirts and work boots.

Never a sign of makeup.

He'd felt bad as she'd walked down the hall in that short white nightdress because he'd looked too hard.

And his body reacted instantly.

The sooner he'd achieved what he'd set out to do, the sooner he could get out of Bindarra Creek. That had been his plan.

The problem was he'd already started to feel comfortable in the town and Grant didn't know if he wanted to leave just yet. He'd been welcomed warmly—tonight at the pub with Ryan and Joe had been enjoyable—and it was true, there was plenty of work here. He'd even had a few enquiries from locals who'd seen the sign on the side of his ute.

Shaking his head in disgust, he cursed Russ Kendall to hell and back.

He'd go and find Mike Potter and sort him out right now.

***

Cathy barely slept after she'd crawled into her double bed with the kids. After being pushed across to the side of the bed as Josie spread across the mattress, and being kept awake by Billy's gentle snores, Cathy climbed out of bed and pulled a spare doona and pillow from the top of the wardrobe.

It was too hot to sleep under the cover; the summer heat had arrived already. She spread the doona on the new carpet and lay on top of it, staring at the moonlight that was reflected on the ceiling. Wide awake, her thoughts turned to the events of the night and a cold chill ran down her back. What if that man had grabbed Josie and she hadn't been able to call for help? She could have slept all night and not missed her daughter until she woke up in the morning. She could have been a long way away . . . or worse.

Cathy regretted not calling the police; Grant hadn't really encouraged her to. She'd take the kids with her and go down to the station tomorrow. It was only two blocks away; maybe she should have called. Maybe one of the policemen there lived in the staff house that Sergeant Bartlett had lived in when she was in high school. Maybe she should have called while the incident was fresh in Josie's mind. But she had been reluctant to call them for other reasons too.

Cathy's face burned. She'd never forget the day that Kevin Strickland called the police sergeant to school to talk to the group of girls Cathy hung around with. Because she sat with them, she had been accused of bullying by association. Nina Potter had been awful at school, and from all accounts, she was still a nasty piece of work. She'd always been jealous of the other girls for some reason or another. Cleo had told her how Nina had deliberately left her off the invitation for the school reunion for their year at the ten-year anniversary of leaving school.

Cleo had heard about it, and come up from Sydney with her friends, Janice and Chrissie, and that's when she and Jon had got together.

She pulled a face as she remembered what Nina had done back then. She'd told Cleo that Jon was with Cathy, and that Billy and Josie were his. Nina was a nasty piece of work and from all accounts was still a troublemaker. She'd worked in various businesses around town, but never lasted very long in any of them. Last she heard Nina was working in the office at the caravan park across the road. Lea had mentioned that some of the cabins there occasionally housed some previous prison inmates.

And that was another reason for Billy to stay away from the river.

Cathy rolled over and tried to close down the thoughts churning in her head, but at three o'clock in the morning, everything seemed so much worse.

Her association with Nina at high school ended after the police sergeant visited the school, and she found the courage to leave the group.

Out of the frying pan into the fire, that had been.

When Cathy had moved away from Nina's group, Russ had asked her to sit with him.

A Year 8 girl sitting with a Year 11 boy had given her status but it had also taken her away from the bullying of Nina and her group for a while.

All of this was ahead for Josie, and all Cathy could hope was that the behaviour of high school kids had improved since she'd been at school. Jaclyn would be a good principal, she was fair and she was savvy, so hopefully she'd have bullying under control.

Cathy lay there for a long time thinking back to those early days with Russ. One thing she would always be grateful for, from the whole sorry mess, was her two beautiful children.

She would do anything to protect them, and anything to make sure they were happy.

Billy had started to talk about Russ lately, and she knew it wouldn't be long before she had to sit down and tell Billy—and Josie—the truth.

Tears crept from her eyes as she lay there, and she wasn't sure what she was crying for. It certainly wasn't because she missed Russ.

It was time to dig deeper for strength and prepare for being a parent of children on the cusp of their teenage years.

As well as honing her parenting skills, she would have to prepare herself financially and emotionally. She would never trust a man again, even though she knew that Billy needed a strong male role model in his life.

He had Uncle Jon, and Ryan, Jaclyn's husband, to look up to.

But Cathy was well aware that Ryan and Jon had their own families and Billy wasn't their responsibility. She tossed and turned as she worried until dawn broke, when she finally fell into a deep sleep.

Chapter 10

Grant was late getting to River Cottage on Monday. After speaking to Mike Potter on Saturday night, and getting nothing out of him, including any admission that it had been him in the backyard of the cottage, he'd warned Potter to stay away, parked his car under the tree across the road from River Cottage and kept an eye on the place all night.

There'd been no more night visitors and no lights had come on inside Cathy's house. He'd left at sunrise, gone home, slept late and then drove to Tamworth at lunchtime.

He went to see Sally, but she claimed she hadn't spoken to Mike again, nor had she known he was out of jail.

'All I want is my share of the money.'

'You don't even know that there's money there,' Grant argued. 'And if there is, it needs to go back to the rightful owners.'

'There is, you know that, and I know that, and I deserve my share. It might be the reason you took off from Bindarra Creek, but I want my share. I am a rightful owner as you put it, Mr Holier-than-thou. It's the least I can do for Beau. If Russ Kendall was still around, I'd get it from him. I might even go and see that Cathy if you don't find that money.'

'Just stay away from Bindarra Creek, Sally. I've got things under control.'

'Have you really, Grant? Or was it just an excuse to set up another branch of your business there? If you'd honestly been going to look for that money, there was no need to go through all that garbage about setting up a branch and building that duplex. I think you were using that as an excuse. Maybe to me, maybe to yourself. You could have just saved the money it cost you to set up and given it to me.'

'Given it to you?' Grant yelled, immediately ashamed of losing his temper. Sally had always known how to push his buttons. He lowered his voice and forced an even tone. 'Give me one good reason why *I* should work to support you, Sally? I have no idea why you left Melbourne. Did Mum and Dad give up on you too?'

Her bottom lip jutted out, just like it had when they were kids. 'You need to help me because I have a child to support.'

'And so do many other women who go out to *work* to support their children. It's about time you got a job. I'm letting you live here rent-free, and you make no effort to find work.' All Grant could think about was what Ryan had said about Cathy. How independent she was and how she refused to take anything from her in-laws. He'd seen for himself how little she had, but he could tell that she was doing a great job of bringing up her two children under difficult circumstances. They were polite and obedient kids and had been genuinely interested in what was happening in the backyard.

He smiled ruefully. Josie's major concern had been the impact of the noise on her rooster.

'I get enough on benefits,' Sally muttered.

'And what a great example that is to Beau.' Grant's frustration increased. 'He's learning that you don't have to make an effort for anything in life. You just sponge on others and get what you want. No wonder he's having trouble at school. He has no work ethic.'

'Well, how about *you* take him and teach him one, seeing you're such a hard worker. He can get a school traineeship and work with you, Uncle Grant.'

Grant nodded. 'If he organises that with the school, *himself*, I'll take him on. But there'll be no slacking off. If he comes to work with me, that's what he'll do. He'll work.'

It was well after eight the next morning when Grant pulled up at the cottage to start work for the day. For some reason, he was nervous about seeing Cathy again.

That was stupid. Maybe it was the guilt that

he wasn't being honest with her, but he would make sure that he spoke to her today and told her that he'd spoken to Mike Potter.

Not that it had done any good. Mike swore black and blue he'd never said anything to Sally about any money, but Grant suspected he was lying through his teeth.

He knew he shouldn't judge by appearance, but these days Mike looked more like a thug than he had in high school. He was covered with tattoos and a scar ran down one side of his face. Both ears held large black discs. His eyes had been cold, and after Grant had challenged him about telling the truth, he'd told him in no uncertain terms to get the hell away from him.

'Morning, Grant.' Joe gave him a cheery wave from the back of the house where his gumboots were splattered with mud. 'Ryan's gone to get the decking from Tamworth. He'll be back at lunchtime. He said if you need a hand to get the fence frame up, I can stop this blasted digging and help you.'

'Thanks, I might take you up on that.'

Grant glanced up at the house as he headed back to the ute to unload the tools he needed today.

All was quiet.

***

'Billy, have you put your geography

homework in your bag?' Cathy called.

'Thanks, Mum. I forgot it.'

Cathy and the kids had spent a quiet day yesterday, getting more of the boxes unpacked and the house organised and doing homework. Even though it had been a clear and warm spring day, Josie was reluctant to go outside, even to feed Red.

After lunch, Cathy took her hand. 'Come on, we'll go outside and get some fresh air, and check on Red.'

'You go, Mummy. I'll finish my picture for school.'

'No, we'll all go out and get some fresh air.'

Josie's eyes filled with tears. 'What if that man comes back?'

'He won't. But how about I take my phone and we can ring Uncle Ryan if anything happens.' Cathy squeezed her hand. 'And it won't, you know. That was just a one-off and it won't happen again. I think that man was just taking a shortcut through our backyard. It's easy because there are so many gaps in the fence. He's probably been doing it for a long time and didn't know we lived here now.'

'You think so?' Josie's face brightened a bit.

'I know so.' Cathy smiled as Josie visibly relaxed. 'Come on, we'll go and check Red's food and water. Come on, Billy. You come too.'

Nothing untoward happened when they

were out there, and they stayed outside in the warm sun for a couple of hours. Cathy walked around the yard pulling weeds from around the old chook pen, and Josie let Red out and followed him around as he scratched for worms.

They stayed away from the building works adjacent to the back of the house as the ground was soft and muddy. When Josie was settled and walking around behind the rooster, Cathy casually wandered over to where Joe had been digging the footing and tried to look for footprints in the churned-up mud.

It was easy to spot their work boot prints from the patterned soles. As Cathy turned to walk back to Josie, her breath caught as she noticed an imprint of a large foot. A bare foot. She glanced across at Josie but she was content wandering around with Red. Billy was over on the vacant block next door and was kicking his football around. She stared at the bare footprint. It was a very large print. Longer than any of the work boot prints around the footings.

She walked closer and followed the prints. Some were clear in the mud, and the puddles obscured some. It looked like whoever it was had walked along the back of the house and then back again. As she reached the edge of the house, the print came close to some smaller footprints.

Obviously, Josie's.

Fear crawled up Cathy's spine as she realised how close the intruder had been to Josie.

Suddenly all she wanted to do was be inside with the children with the door locked safely behind them.

'Billy, come back home now,' she called. 'Josie, we'll go in and you can help me make a cake, so you've got something for recess tomorrow.'

The afternoon had passed uneventfully, and once the chocolate cake was in the oven and the kids were settled in front of the television, Cathy went out to the front porch and called Jaclyn.

Her friend picked up the call immediately.

'Hi Cathy, great timing. I was just about to call you. I was going to this morning, but we had to go to Tamworth. Georgia's just gone down for a nap, and I literally just picked up the phone. What was wrong last night?'

Cathy quickly explained what had happened.

'Did you call the police station?'

'No.'

'Why not?'

'I figured they couldn't do anything.' She lowered her voice. 'I told Josie it was probably someone taking a shortcut but I'm not so sure now. I just found some footprints around the back of the house.'

'I'm coming to town for a meeting tomorrow morning. How about we have coffee when I'm done, and I'll come to the police station with you?'

'I think I will,' Cathy said slowly. 'Maybe there's been some break and enters in town. Poor little Josie is still nervy. I'll drive the kids to school tomorrow and come home and wait for your call.'

'Okay, talk to you about one. Lunch at the pub?'

'Sounds good.' Cathy thought about how much cash she had. A toastie wouldn't cost much.

Cathy walked to the car after checking again that Billy had packed his homework.

'Yes, Mum. Don't nag.'

Once the kids had climbed in, she glanced over her shoulder. 'I'll be out for lunch with Aunty Jac this afternoon, so I'll pick you up. Okay?'

Billy caught her eye in the rear vision mirror, and she knew he was old enough to understand why she was going to pick them up.

Josie held her tight as she walked her to the primary school gate. 'You be careful today, Mummy.'

'It's fine, sweetie. Uncle Ryan and Joe and Mr Cummings will all be working in the yard today.'

When she parked the car at the side of the house, Joe was already in the backyard holding the shovel, and Grant was carrying some posts through the gap in the side fence.

'Morning,' she said as she walked over. Grant put the posts on the ground.

'How are you all, Cathy?'

She nodded. 'We're fine. But I'll go to the police station later today. I noticed some suspicious footprints here yesterday afternoon.'

'Suspicious?' Joe's eyes widened. 'What happened?'

'We had an intruder in the yard on Saturday night. Josie got a big fright.'

Joe let out a low whistle. 'Not good. Anything taken? Any damage?'

'No. Just a scare. But I was thinking maybe we shouldn't disturb these until the police come to take a look.' She gestured to the footprints near the three holes Joe had dug last week.

'That sounds sensible. I can work at the other end today. Anything I can do to help, you just yell out, Cathy.'

'Thanks, Joe.' As she turned to go back to the house, Grant fell into step beside her.

'How's Josie?'

'She's coming good.'

'Good. No more issues over the weekend?'

'No.'

He walked beside her as though he wanted to say more. She waited for him to speak.

'Was there something else you needed me for, Grant?' Cathy frowned when he hesitated for a minute and then shook his head.

'No. No, just checking you were all okay.'

Cathy was cross with herself because she felt as though she owed Grant for looking after them on Saturday night.

She hadn't asked him to, and she still wondered why he'd been driving past on Saturday night. River Cottage was not between the pub and his apartment a hundred metres down the road. She wondered if he remembered her from school, but he hadn't indicated that, so she wasn't going to say anything. He'd been in Russ's year, and she was sure he'd been around some of the time when she had come onto Russ's radar when she was in Year 8.

She owed Grant nothing, and if she fell into the trap of getting someone to look after them less than a day after she'd moved out to prove her independence, she'd failed miserably.

'We're fine,' she said shortly and hurried up the front steps, not looking at him before she unlocked the door, went inside and closed it behind her.

An hour later, guilt got the better of Cathy. She quickly cooked a batch of pikelets, buttered them and put them on a plate, before covering them with a teatowel and going downstairs.

'Hi guys, it must be close to smoko by now. I've made you some pikelets.'

Grant looked across at her and she gave him a tentative smile by way of an apology for her earlier rudeness.

Putting the plate on a stump in the middle of the yard near the clothesline, she called out to Joe and Ryan.

'Have you got your flasks, or do you want me to make a coffee for you?'

'No, thanks, Cath. It's okay,' Ryan said. 'We've got our smoko in the back of my ute, but I won't say no to a fresh pikelet.'

'What about you, Grant?'

'I'm fine,' he said, picking up a post.

Before he headed off to the fence line, she reached out and touched his arm. 'No, I'll make you a cuppa. What would you prefer? Tea or coffee?' she asked.

He stopped and looked at her intently. Cathy relaxed as his face creased in a smile.

'A cup of tea would be great, thanks. White with one.' He put the post down and walked over to where Joe was perusing the plate of pikelets.

'Help yourselves,' Cathy said. 'They don't keep.'

She hurried upstairs into the kitchen and was back outside within minutes carrying a coffee for herself and a cup of tea for Grant.

'Jac was telling me about your excitement here on Saturday night,' Ryan said. 'Have you got any more ideas about who it was?'

'No, but I'm meeting Jaclyn when she finishes her meeting at the school; she offered to come to the police station with me. She said there's been a few break and enters around town over the last couple of weeks.'

'Yes, there have been.' Ryan gestured with his thumb across the road. 'I hate to say it and I hate to be judgemental, but there have been a few dodgy characters living in the caravan park lately. Mike Potter would've been in your year at school, wouldn't he, Grant? He's about our age.'

Cathy widened her eyes wondering how Grant would react. As far as he was aware she hadn't recognised him from their school days and didn't know he'd been a local.

Grant held her eye as he spoke. 'Yes, Mike Potter is pretty suss. He lives in the caravan park.'

'Do you think he could be responsible?' Ryan reached for another pikelet.

'What for?' Cathy asked. 'Coming on to our

property or the break and enters?'

Ryan shrugged. 'Who knows? I don't like to accuse out of line, but I've pretty much found where there's smoke there's usually fire. And in a small town like this, not a lot stays under the radar.'

'But being a local, he'd know that surely? If he was going to go somewhere to do those sorts of things, why would he pick Bindarra Creek?' Joe said.

Cathy nodded.

Especially a town where he was well-known and recognisable.

As the guys quickly demolished the plate of pikelets, she looked around, surprised to see the progress they'd made on the fence.

On one side of the yard—the side that backed onto the vacant block—one whole section of cream Colourbond panels had been secured. Another half-length had been completed behind the chook shed.

'Wow, you've had a big morning already and it's only ten o'clock. It really makes the yard private, doesn't it?' Cathy commented.

'Yes, once it's finished it will give you a private and sheltered area at the back of the house.' Ryan gestured with his cup. 'But the deck'll be high enough that you'll still be able to see the street over the fence.'

'It's going to look different when it's finished.'

'We hope to have the structure done by next weekend. You'll be able to come out the back and stand on it, hopefully by Friday,' Ryan said. 'We've stopped work on it today to give Grant a hand with the fence. Grant bought a lock at the hardware so you can lock the gate and get your car in there at night, and you'll be able to go in the back door.'

'And next time I go to Tamworth, I'll bring back a remote control so you won't have to get out to the car to lock and unlock the gate.'

Cathy smiled at their thoughtfulness. 'Is this all because of Saturday night?'

'We want you to be safe in town, Cathy, and to feel safe too,' Grant said.

'Make sure you bill me for the lock and the remote,' Cathy replied. 'I really appreciate your help. All of you.' She looked past Grant to include Ryan and Joe.

'Not a problem, Cathy.' Joe walked over and looked at the footprints they had left untouched today. 'Another reason we helped Grant today was because of the water in the holes. I had to stop digging on Friday because there's so much groundwater from the recent rain. I couldn't see what I hit down there. There's bricks or concrete at the bottom of the second hole on the street side.

Ryan's decided we'll bring a pump tomorrow and pump out the water in case it's the foundations of the house or a concrete water pipe.'

'You guys know what you're doing. I'll leave you to it.'

Cathy reached over and took Grant's cup from his hand and as her fingers brushed his, an unfamiliar tingle ran up her arm. Heat ran up into her face from her neck, and she looked down when she realised Grant was staring at her.

'I'll see you all later.' She hurried inside, and when she realised she'd left the pikelet plate outside, she didn't go back for it.

Chapter 11

'Billy? Did you hang your towel up? Or did you leave it on the bathroom floor?' Cathy walked down the hallway towards the bathroom.

'Left it.' Billy shot past her. 'I'm just going to hang it up now, Mum.'

Cathy rolled her eyes. Typical boy, Billy never put anything where it was supposed to go, and she'd just about given up on teaching him. She could hear herself; she was turning into the nag he'd called her this morning.

'I had my shower, Mummy, and I hung my towel up.' Josie's sweet voice came from her bedroom.

'Thank you, sweetie. I'll have to get you to teach Billy how to clean up after himself.'

'I had homework to do.' Billy stopped at the bathroom door. 'I have high school homework. Josie's doesn't matter.'

'Everyone's homework matters.' Cathy stood in Josie's doorway. 'Fifteen minutes and then lights out for you, Billy. Josie, bed for you now.' She walked across to the bed and leaned down to kiss Josie, smiling as a pair of warm little arms went around her neck.

112

'Love you, Mummy.'

'I love you too.'

'And I love my new bed and my *Frozen* bedspread.'

'That's good. Okay with the light out? I'll leave the hall light on.'

'Hall light is good.' Josie put on an exaggerated yawn and snuggled down in her bed. She seemed a lot less nervous tonight.

Cathy went back to the kitchen and wiped down the benches. She was enjoying being in a home with just herself and the kids—even if Billy and Josie did fight. They'd always been on their best behaviour at Lea and David's, and she grinned now. They were both relaxing in their new home environment and both seemed happy living in town.

Flicking the kettle on, she crossed to the window. She could see the new fence from the kitchen window; the three men had finished it just before dinner time. Grant had called her out to put her car away and he'd handed her the key when she came out the gate. She closed and locked it, and smiled at him.

'Thank you.'

'My pleasure,' he said abruptly. 'See you in a couple of days. I'll bring the remote. He turned on his heel and went out to his ute. Cathy stood there as he drove away without a backward glance.

And why should he? He was a tradesman, not a friend.

Cathy knew she was attracted to Grant, but it was only because he'd been so helpful.

So have Ryan and Joe, said a little voice in her head.

And he was a good-looking man. That's all it was.

He was secretive and what did she really know about him? Why hadn't he come right out and said to her, *I was at school the same time as you. I was friends with Russ.*

Or would he say, I was friends with the father of your children? Your missing partner? Your dead partner?

Cathy put a halt on the direction her thoughts were taking.

It was a new start. She would forget about the past, and focus on the future.

First job tomorrow: look at the positions vacant in town, and ask Jaclyn what she needed to get together so she was ready to apply for the school job when it came up.

She put the gate keys in her pocket and went upstairs to cook dinner. When she reached the end of the driveway she looked back at the new fence. Solid and secure, and private.

Josie would be ecstatic; Red could now

wander at will. Grant had fenced off a small enclosure in the corner of the yard near the temporary chook shed.

As soon as the deck was finished, Cathy intended prettying it up. She'd seen some second-hand wicker outdoor furniture at the back of Dodge's shop and had paid a deposit. As it was coming into summer, she'd go to the nursery and buy a couple of tubs and fill them with some bright annuals. In the short time they'd lived here when Billy was a baby, she'd taken pleasure in growing her vegetables and flowers.

But this time her flowers would thrive.

She pushed open the front door, but the past memories wouldn't leave her alone. Maybe it was healthier to revisit them and know that she was now safe.

The children were safe and wouldn't ever know what sort of man their father had been.

Russ had come home early one afternoon and destroyed her garden. She'd been five months pregnant with Josie and had gone outside while Billy had a late afternoon sleep. Losing track of the time, she'd not put dinner on, and it happened to be the one time Russ came home early from his afternoon at the pub. When he saw her in the garden, he'd calmly walked over and without looking at her or touching her, he'd methodically pulled out every row of plants, and then tipped out the hanging baskets that she'd hung from a wire underneath the back of the house.

'Now you'll have time to make sure dinner is on the table when I get home,' he'd yelled as he pushed her up the back steps.

The next day, Cathy had gone to see her parents and begged them to let her and Billy come home, but the reception had been cold.

'You made your bed, girl. You'll put up with it. And a man is entitled to have his dinner on the table when he gets home,' her father had said. Mum and Dad had moved away a few months later; and she'd never seen them again.

Lethargy filled her as she walked past the living room where the kids were watching television, and down to the kitchen. As she peeled pumpkin and potatoes, her eyes filled.

What chance did Billy and Josie have to grow up well-adjusted? A thug for a father, and no one knew where he was, for sure.

Her mood brightened as she listened to the happy chatter of the kids at the dinner table. She was worrying unnecessarily.

They were good kids and she'd make sure they'd have every chance in life.

Forcing herself to be positive and think about the garden she'd plant out, she made herself a cup of tea. Heading into the living room she looked with satisfaction at the small table and chairs setting she and Jaclyn had found at Dodge and Tessa's place today. They'd gone to the police station first and left a message with the constable on the front desk. He'd promised that someone would come to see her as soon as they could. Dodge had put the furniture on the truck and bought it around straight away.

'That Ryan Rossiter's a mover, that's for sure. The place is looking great,' he said admiring the freshly-painted interior as he carried the table in. 'Welcome to town, Cathy. Don't hesitate to ask if you need a hand with anything, although it looks like Ryan has the job under control.' Dodge stood on the front porch chatting for a while. 'Work's picking up in town. I've got a quite a few jobs lined up at the moment.'

'Life's getting back to normal after a difficult time,' Cathy said.

'Yep, between COVID and the floods, the last couple of years have been tough out here in the bush. But look, blue skies now and the weather's warming up, and Christmas is just around the corner. Bindarra Creek is coming to life again.'

She and Jaclyn ended up having a sandwich at the cottage instead of buying lunch at the pub. Cathy had enjoyed showing her around.

'Ryan and Joe are amazing. I can't believe how fast they work.'

'And what about Grant?' Cathy didn't like the way Jaclyn was looking at her.

'What about Grant? Yes, he's a good worker too.'

'Not bad looking either.' This time Jaclyn smiled.

'Don't start, Jac.'

'It's about time you had a life, Cathy.'

'I have a very nice life, and now I have my own place, it's going to get even better.'

'Okay, I won't harp, but Ryan's planning on having a barbie soon. Will you come? And the kids, of course.'

'Just let me know when, and we'll be there.'

Jaclyn left when Cathy headed out to pick the kids up. She was feeling restless, so she left the car at home and walked across to the school; the primary and high school were only four blocks away. Josie chatted about her day all the way home, and Billy stopped at the tennis courts and the pool.

'Can I join the swim club, Mum? And maybe tennis on Friday afternoons?'

'I'll see. It depends on how much it costs.'

Billy dropped his head and scuffed his shoes all the way home.

Now Cathy put her cup of tea on the floor

and settled into the bean bag. Billy could have ten more minutes and then she'd find a movie she wanted to watch.

Smiling, she picked up the remote and contentment stole over her. It was only a small part of living here but it was *her* remote. She could choose what she wanted to watch after the kids were in bed. Once her tea was finished, she put her head back and closed her eyes.

'How much longer, Mum?' Billy called out a while later.

Cathy jumped; she must have dozed off. She glanced at the small clock on the TV stand, and pushed herself out of the bean bag.

'I'm coming. Another two minutes.'

Billy hated being tucked in, but she still made sure she got a kiss and a hug from him every night. He was a good kid, and she could put up with the wet towels on the floor and the lid off the toothpaste. She just wished that money wasn't so tight. She'd start looking for a job tomorrow so that Billy could join the swim squad and the tennis club.

When Russ had left, she'd always been terrified that not having a dad would impact the kids. She'd also worried that he'd passed his mean streak on, but so far so good. They were both polite and obedient children and cared for other people. Josie loved her animals, and Billy was a considerate

119

player in all his team sports at school. Russ had been an excellent sportsman, but he'd been a thug on the football field, bragging when he'd been responsible for a tackle that sent an opposing player off injured.

At almost thirteen, Billy was a well-adjusted and good kid.

Detouring via the kitchen Cathy put the cup and saucer on the sink and frowned as a shadow crossed the kitchen window. Walking across, she peered out, but there was nothing to see. The moonlight shone brightly on the vacant paddock next door; it must have been a bird or a flying fox.

Her blood turned to ice as Josie's scream pierced the silence.

Cathy ran.

Chapter 12

For some reason, Grant found it hard to settle after he'd finished dinner. Even though it had been early evening when they'd left River Cottage, the Cyprus Café was still open and he'd got takeaway moussaka for dinner. Thea Levonis' cooking was still legendary. He couldn't believe they still ran the café; they'd been there when he was a teenager.

Ryan had headed out to his property, keen to get home before his little girl had gone to bed, and Joe had a hot date with some girl who'd just moved back to town.

Grant raised his eyebrows. 'A Monday night date? You must be keen.'

Joe chuckled. 'Two lonely people and dinner at the Riverside Pub. I'm staying at Ryan and Jac's, but I like to give them space.' His grin was wide. 'And if a pretty woman agrees to have dinner with me, who am I to say no?'

'A local, you said?'

'Yeah, I met Leah at the pub the other night. She's moved back to town from Sydney. Going to live here and illustrate children's books.'

'Good to see the town growing,' Grant said.

'Yep, there'll be more work for everyone, and good for the town economy. While I think of it, Grant, are you going to rent out the other side of your duplex?'

Grant shook his head. 'Not yet, mate. Depends on how long I stay in town. But I'll let you know as soon as I decide. Is she looking for somewhere to stay?'

'No, I am. I'd rather live in town, now that I'm working locally. It was okay living out at Ryan and Jac's farm between shearing jobs, but they need their space. Plus, I've picked up a couple of bar shifts at the Riverside Pub, so it'd be good to live in town.'

'I'll let you know as soon as I can.'

'Thanks, mate. Appreciate it.'

Grant was restless when he got home. He ate his dinner, and watched the ABC news, and then looked at his watch.

It was too soon to go to bed. He'd go for a walk, and then when he got home, he'd call Sally and see if Beau had done anything about a school traineeship.

Grant walked for two hours, reacquainting himself with Bindarra Creek. It was still light for the first half of his walk, and he strolled past the sports oval where he'd played many games of football. Cutting across the paddocks, he came to the back of Fred's garage where he'd had his first paid job pumping fuel.

Russ couldn't understand why he wanted a job, and Grant had explained that his parents needed the money.

'But do you get to keep some for yourself?' Russ had asked with a grin. 'I can tell you where we can get some good hooch.'

Grant had gotten out of it by telling him his parents took it all. He'd seen what drugs had done to his cousin, Brian. He'd started off on dope and then got into the hard stuff and ended up in jail. He wasn't going down that track.

He crossed Main Street and walked back towards the main part of town. He could still remember the day they'd driven into Bindarra Creek in Dad's Commodore, Grant, a sullen teenager in the back seat, Sally beside him, whining about the move to the bush. They'd come from Sydney where the streets were always busy and people were always outside.

They'd driven into Bindarra Creek on a Sunday afternoon, and wondered where everyone was. They hadn't passed a single car or person outside until they reached the post office where Dad was the new postmaster.

A man had been mowing the footpath outside the strip of shops. He remembered Mum had commented on the coloured daisies that were going under the mower.

'What a shame, they were pretty,' she'd said.

Sally had muttered beside him in the back seat. 'What is this place? It's like something from a sci-fi movie. Everyone's been beamed up.'

But Grant had settled in, even if it had been with the wrong group.

He reached the corner of Church and Main and debated which way to go. He turned left and headed towards River Cottage in the dark.

It wouldn't hurt to walk past and check everything was all right. He glanced at his watch; he'd been walking two hours and darkness had fallen. There was no moon, but the streetlights gave off enough light to see where he was going.

He looked across at the caravan park when he turned onto River Road, but there was no sign of life. Lights were on in a couple of the cabins and two caravans were parked near the amenities block, but no one was out and about.

As he walked closer to town, Grant stayed on the river side of the road. He'd hate for Cathy to look out and think he was spying on her.

He worried about her; for some reason, she'd touched him, and he found her coming into his thoughts a lot during the day.

And night.

Grant shook himself mentally; it was just that he was working on the job at her house. Once they'd finished, he'd forget about her.

For a moment, he forgot the real reason he was here and that surprised him.

He had settled into Bindarra Creek in the short time he'd been here. He liked the people, and he was enjoying the work; he'd had a constant stream of enquiries over the past few days.

He shoved his hands in his pockets and kept his head down until he was past Cathy's house. The lights were out and there was no sign of life.

It was a bloody shame she'd moved in as soon as he'd arrived in town. If she'd been a week later, he could have had a good poke around the house and found what he was looking for—or what Sally wanted him to find. As it was now, he wasn't prepared to do that, and he'd be telling Sally that this weekend.

Grant strode out and headed for his apartment; he'd do up some quotes tonight before he went to bed and forget about Cathy Kendall and what could be buried in her backyard.

He hoped there was nothing there and Sally would leave him in peace.

Chapter 13

Cathy flew down the hall and into Josie's room, her heart pounding so hard it hurt.

'Mummy, Mummy, the shiny man's at my window.' Josie's face was white, and her little hand shook as she pointed to the window. 'He tapped on the window, and he looked at me, Mummy. He's come back to get me. He's got funny pointy teeth.'

Cathy hurried over to the window and looked out but there was nothing to be seen. The light from the streetlight on the corner lit up the side of the house, and the narrow walkway was deserted.

As was the street.

'Sweetheart, it was just a little nightmare because it's too high for anyone to look in. It's too far from the ground.'

'It was just his shiny head and his face, Mummy. I *saw* him. I really and truly saw him. I wasn't asleep.'

'It was a nightmare, sweetheart. Sometimes dreams can seem very real.'

Josie lifted the blanket and stared at Cathy. 'I wasn't asleep.' She pulled out a book and a torch from under the covers. 'I was being naughty, but I really wanted to finish my book. I was reading and I

126

heard someone tapping on the window and I looked over and he was there, and he pulled a scary face at me. I saw his pointy teeth. Honestly, Mummy, I saw him, and then he pointed at me. That's when I screamed.'

Cathy reached up and smoothed Josie's hair. 'It's okay, sweetie. I'll go outside and have a look.'

Josie grabbed her hand and held it tightly. 'No, Mummy, you won't go out. He might hurt you and then I'll have no Mummy or Daddy.' Her voice was shrill and on the verge of hysteria. 'Don't go!'

Billy appeared in the doorway. 'What's wrong now?'

'It's okay, mate. You go back to bed. Josie was just having a bad dream.'

'I wasn't. Promise you won't go outside.'

'Okay, darling. I promise. I'll have a look in the morning. Okay?'

Cathy sat beside Josie, smoothing her hair as an occasional shiver shook her little body. Finally, she drifted off, and Billy went back to his room. When Cathy was sure Josie was sound asleep, she got up and checked the window was locked and then took another look outside. When she went into Billy's room, he was asleep too. She turned out all the lights and systematically went through the house and looked out all the windows as she checked they were locked. The only fresh air coming into the house was through the high toilet window which was too small for anyone to climb in.

The backyard was empty, and she felt more secure because Grant and Ryan had finished the fence late this afternoon. The side gate was locked, and the key was in her pocket. What did worry her a little was that the side of the house where the bedrooms were was on the outer side of the new fence. On that side, it was in a line with the back of the house. Tomorrow she'd ask Grant to extend it and take it right to the front of the house. She had enough put away so she could pay for that.

As Cathy went to pull down the blind at the living room window, her breath caught in a stifled gasp. Her blood turned to ice as a tall man— a huge man with his bald head shining in the streetlight— walked up the front path. His feet thudded on the timber front steps as he headed up the steps towards the front door. Cathy stepped to the side of the window but kept her eyes on him as she reached into her pocket for her phone.

Ryan was too far away. Maybe she should call triple zero, but she knew Grant was the closest. Her fingers wrapped around the gate key that Grant had given her after she put the car away, but there was no phone. She'd put the phone down on the floor in Josie's bedroom when she'd been smoothing her hair and forgotten it when she'd left the room.

Cathy backed away from the window as a loud knock sounded on the front door. With her heart in her throat, she bit her lip, not knowing what to do. Whether to pretend they weren't there, or they were asleep, but if he'd been hanging around, he would have seen the lights on a few minutes ago.

Josie must have seen him. He must have really been at her window.

What the hell did he want?

Pushing her shaking hands into her jeans pockets, Cathy walked to the door and checked that the deadlock was on. It was secure and she took a deep breath.

'Who is it?' she said forcing a normal tone, and firmness and confidence into her voice.

'Oh gidday, ma'am. I was wondering if you could open the side gate for me. I think my dog got underneath your fence. He's in your backyard.'

Cathy stood still and waited a moment.

'No, it can't get in there. We have a new fence, and it goes right to the ground, so no dog can get under it,' she said. 'It must have gone somewhere else.' She wasn't going to tell him that under the house was unfenced.

'Can you open the door please? I need to talk to you,' he said.

Cathy frowned as she tried to remember if

she'd locked the screen door when she came in earlier; not that that would do any good if she opened the door. She'd be more vulnerable.

'Open the door.' The deep voice was less pleasant. Cathy stood perfectly still and listened. 'I need help, I'm hurt. Please help me.'

He was lying, trying to use any excuse to get her to open the door. Cathy gripped her hands tightly; she was ninety-nine percent sure she'd locked the screen door when she came in. It was something she just did automatically without thinking.

When Lea had the screens and doors replaced last week, the company had come over from Tamworth and installed Crim safe screens.

Cathy had said it was a waste of money in Bindarra Creek, but now she was pleased that Lea had insisted. If the door was locked, she'd be safe from him.

She swallowed.

Unless he had a gun.

Now she was being melodramatic.

She turned on the outside light and clicked the deadlock over with her hand ready to turn the key in the security door if it wasn't locked.

The door opened and her eyes dropped to the lock in the screen door. The key was in the lock and the silver tab was turned to the lock position.

She lifted her gaze and encountered the steely gaze of a huge man with—God forbid—a *bald, shiny* head.

He was huge; she had to look up a long way. He wore black jeans and a black T-shirt with a motorcycle club emblem on the front. His arms were covered with tattoos that came out of the opening of his T-shirt and continued up his neck.

'What do you want?' she asked, her voice cold. 'I have no money here, and nothing valuable,

'I don't need *your* money. I need to get in your backyard, love.'

'No.'

His mouth twisted and she could see the anger in his expression through the dark screen.

'Yes.'

'No.'

He took a step closer to the door and she instinctively stepped back. 'Okay let's cut to the chase. I am going into your backyard. Now.'

Cathy stared at him, and said slowly. 'Michael Potter.'

'Clever lady.'

Michael had been a fairly weedy kid at school, but he'd grown into a giant of a man. His teeth were, as Josie had said—filed to points—and the sight of him was fearsome to Cathy. No wonder Josie had been terrified.

'Now, I'm not here to cause any trouble. I just need to have a bit of a poke around.' He moved closer to the door. 'Now that you know who I am, we might have to get a little bit serious. Don't you go thinking about calling the police or anything silly like that, will you, sweetheart?'

'Why would I do that, Michael? What do you want? You were a bully at school, but don't think you can bully me now. Anyway, it's too late. I've already been to the police station and reported somebody poking around my yard the other night.'

He laughed. 'Sure gave that little girl of yours a fright though.'

'It was you, the other night?' She played dumb. 'Why were you in my yard? Why do you need to go there now?'

'Look, lovely, it's nothing to concern you. I'm just after something that belongs to me.'

'And if I say no?' Cathy's temper was building. Michael Potter *had* been a bully at school, and she'd hated being with Russ when Michael was hanging around, but she wasn't going to let him bully her now, no matter what a fearsome sight he might be. She was angry that he had frightened Josie.

His next words sent ice trickling through her veins.

'Be a shame if you did, because you know

132

how scared your little girl is of me.' He laughed again and Cathy stared at him.

'You should've seen her face when I looked in the window before. She's a cute little girl.' He smiled, but it wasn't pleasant. 'You do know what can happen to little girls these days? I've got contacts, contacts that would find a nice new home for her. Then again. Maybe not so nice.'

Nausea roiled in Cathy's stomach and a sour taste filled her mouth. Josie hadn't been dreaming. It was easy to see how he would've been able to look through the window just standing at ground level; he had to be about six-five now.

'Right. I'll do what you ask. What do you want?'

'It's simple, love. I just want to have a bit of a look around your backyard. No need to bother you. Just unlock the gate and let me in.'

'I'm not coming out there,' Cathy said. 'How can I trust you?'

She cringed when he burst out laughing. 'You've turned into a smart woman, Cath. Because you're right, you can't trust me. A few years inside will do that to a man.' He leaned forward and pressed his face against the Crim Safe screen. 'Did it do it to Russ, too?' His voice dropped to a gravelly whisper.

'What are you talking about?'

'Don't play dumb with me, bitch. Your bloody man double-crossed me before we even got locked up, and now I'm getting my share back. How about you just pass me the key to that friggin' gate and I won't have to hurt you.'

'I don't trust you,' she said. 'And I will not risk my kids.'

'Jesus, woman, all I want now is the key. Stuff your kids. I'll stand back and you can put it on the floor if you're so worried about me touching you.' He looked her up and down and there was a lascivious smile on his face. 'You've turned into a good-looking girl, Cathy. Never had boobs like that when we were at school. Did Russ pay for them?'

Cathy crossed her arms over her breasts—her *own*—and didn't move.

'So, the key?' he said.

'What did you mean about Russ then?' she asked.

'He ain't coming back, love. And don't play dumb with me. I know very well you know where he is. Amazing what a couple of local fellas will talk about in jail. The days are long and lonely.'

Cathy's heart was pounding, but she didn't move. She didn't know what to do.

'You've got to the count of ten to hand the keys over. If you don't, I might just have to go and see your little girl. Windows break easily, you

134

know. Did you know the senior sarge got called out to the national park tonight? He's a long way from town, Cathy.'

'No, stop. I'll give it to you. Just do what you have to do and then get the hell off my place.'

'I heard it was Lea and David's place, and you're just freeloading. That's the talk around town, anyways.'

Cathy ignored his jibe. If it was true, she didn't care. All she wanted was for him to go away, and the kids to be safe.

'Go and wait at the bottom of the steps and I'll open the door. I'll put the key there, and then when you finish you bring it back. You are not to keep the key.'

'Sweetheart, where I've come from, I don't need a key to get wherever I want. I just don't have time tonight. Russ and I learned some new skills in Sydney. One thing he learned better than me. Do you know what that is?'

Cathy shook her head.

'Russell learnt how to disappear. And he's done a bloody good job of it. Me? I'm a homebody. I'm gonna build myself a flash house out with all the rich people on Mt Ingalls Road.'

'What do you know about Russ?' Cathy could barely get the words out. She didn't know if he was big-noting himself, but if Michael Potter knew anything about Russ, she wanted to know what it was.

'Just between you and me, love, Russell isn't coming back. Don't you worry, he won't be back to bother you. He's found himself a new woman and that's all I'm saying. Now for frig's sake, give me that bloody key. I don't want to stand around and chat with you all night.'

'Go down the stairs and wait,' she said.

'Oh, just one more thing, lovely Cathy.' He tipped his head to the side. 'I might just come back and pay you a visit one night. We could have a drink. Have a bit of fun.'

'Over my dead body. Just stay the hell away from me and my kids. Or—'

'Or what? Or you'll call the police?'

'If I have to.'

His eyes narrowed and his mouth was an ugly slash in his pock-marked face. 'If you tell anyone, including Riley Morgan, I was here, I'll come back for your little girl. Do you hear me?'

Cathy stood, frozen with fear, and nodded mutely.

'Good, now get that bloody key. Don't you tell anybody that I've been here tonight or tell anyone that I've been looking in your backyard. I might have to come back, so don't lock that gate again.' He paused as he turned to go down the steps.

'Oh, and do you know I live just across the road there? I have a perfect view of your house from my place, and I'll see if any cops turn up. Right?'

She nodded.

'And I know you've got two kids and I know what school they go to. You can't watch them all day long. You gotta sleep sometime. No cops.'

'No police, I promise. Please take what you want, and just leave us alone.' Cathy's breath caught and for a minute she thought she was going to faint. 'I don't . . . don't ever want to see you here again.'

'No need to be nasty, sweetheart.'

'I won't say anything more to the police, or anybody else.' She knew if she told Jaclyn and Ryan or Lea and David what had happened tonight, they would have her straight down to the police station.

He grunted and lumbered down the steps and stood there looking up at her. His face was shadowed in the dim moonlight and his gaze stayed on her unblinkingly as she took the gate key from her pocket.

When Cathy was certain that he couldn't get up the steps she quickly unlocked the door and threw the gate key to the floor outside. She relocked the screen door, slammed shut the front door and turned the deadlock with shaking hands. Putting her back against the door, she slid down to a sitting position because her legs wouldn't support her. Panting in ragged breaths, tears spilled from her eyes and ran down her cheeks.

She wasn't going to tell a soul what had happened. All those things he threatened for Josie and Billy made her physically ill; she knew they weren't idle threats. For the first time in many years, Cathy longed for a partner to lean on. Someone who could share the burden and support her and tell her what to do.

She was so tired of being alone.

Why the hell had she agreed to come back to the cottage? She would never feel safe here again.

She wanted to be safe out on the farm living a slow and comfortable, even boring, life, but she knew those days were gone. As soon as she got a job and saved enough, she and the kids would be moving to a town a long way away where no one could find them.

Not Russ, not Michael Potter, not Lea and David.

No one.

It was time to make a new life.

Chapter 14

Cathy didn't sleep at all.

She'd stayed at the door for over an hour waiting for *him* to put the key back on the porch. It had seemed like hours until his heavy tread coming up the steps shook the front of the timber house. There was a muffled noise and then his footsteps went back down the steps. She guessed it was the sound of the key on the porch, but there was no way she was going outside to get it. The gate could stay unlocked.

Curiosity got the better of her and she pushed herself up and hurried to the front window. A tall figure was crossing the road to the caravan park, and she knew it was Michael Potter. His shining head was a dead giveaway. He was carrying something big, but it was too dark to see what it was.

She didn't care. Whatever it was, he could have it. As long as he left them alone.

She wondered if Grant had anything to do with him. He'd been friends with Russ and Michael at school. It seemed coincidental that both of them had come back to town at the same time.

And Grant had never once mentioned who

he was to her.

He had been kind to her, but distant most of the time, and she always had the impression that he was watching and looking.

If he had a big landscaping business with branches all over the state like Joe had told her the other afternoon, why would he be building a fence and garden boxes in a little cottage in Bindarra Creek? Surely, he had employees to do that sort of thing?

Cathy trusted few people, and from today, that would include everyone until she could get herself and the kids out of this town. If only she had enough money.

The toilet flushed up the hall, and then she heard Billy telling Josie to hurry up in the bathroom. Cathy dragged herself out of bed, surprised to see she was still in the same clothes she'd had on yesterday. All she could remember from last night was the fear that had consumed her and she still had that sour taste in her mouth. She waited until she heard the bathroom door open, grabbed a change of clothes and took a hot shower, trying to wash away the feeling of dread that wouldn't leave her.

When she reached the kitchen, the normality of the morning routine calmed her a little. Both the kids were eating cereal; Billy was glued to his iPad as he ate, and Josie was reading her book.

'Morning, munchkins.' Her voice was husky and she cleared her throat.

'Have you got a sore voice, Mummy?' Josie asked.

'No sweetie, I'm just a bit tired, I didn't sleep very well.'

'Did you dream about the scary man?'

'No.' She forced a smile. 'I hope you didn't either.'

'What scary man? The one from the other night?' Billy said.

'Yes.' Josie nodded. 'But I'm not scared anymore. He's gone, hasn't he, Mummy? I imagined him at my window last night, Billy, but like Mummy said, my window is too high. It was all in my imagination.'

Cathy dropped a kiss on top of both of their heads on her way to the sink to fill the kettle.

She wanted to warn the kids to be careful, but at the same time, she didn't want to scare them. They were both too young to have to deal with what had happened last night. All she could hope and pray for was that he'd found what he was looking for and would leave them in peace.

She stood at the window sipping an extra strong cup of coffee and thinking about the day ahead. Best thing to do would be to keep the kids home from school until she was sure that everything was safe.

'How would you like to stay home from school today?' she said brightly.

Billy frowned and looked at her as though she had two heads. 'Why?'

'Keep me company.'

Josie looked at Billy and wrinkled her nose, and then looked at Cathy. 'Are you sure you're not sick, Mummy?'

'I'm fine.'

'I can't stay home. I've got cricket practice at lunchtime. If we don't turn up every lunchtime, we lose our chance of getting picked for the team,' Billy said with his mouth full.

'And I've got sewing this afternoon.' Josie stood and took her plate over to the sink. 'We're making a stuffed frog for a toy. I'm going to give it to Aunty Cleo for the new baby. Can we go out there on Saturday?'

Cathy nodded. 'Okay. I guess it's good you both want to go to school. But a special treat today. I'll drive you and after school, I'll pick you up and we'll go to the café for a milkshake.'

Billy and Josie looked at each other again, and Cathy knew she'd have to try harder to be normal. She forced a laugh.

'What, am I such a horrible mum that a

milkshake treat isn't normal?'

'Well,' Billy said. 'We know we can't afford lots of treats.'

'Well, that's all changing. I'm going to get a job, and we'll have more money for milkshakes and treats.'

'Pizza?' Billy said hopefully. 'At the Riverside Pub?'

Cathy nodded again and laughed. 'We'll go on Friday night.'

'Can I invite Eddie Taylor for tea and a sleepover?' Billy looked at her sideways. 'He could check out the river here to see if we can get the kayaks in.'

'Yes, you can ask him, but we'll see about the river. Josie, would you like to invite a friend too?'

'No, I can play with Eddie too. I like him.'

'No, you can't, he's my friend.' Billy glared at her.

'Okay, you pair, go and brush your teeth and pack your bags. You can have canteen money today.'

'Way to go, Mum.' Billy threw her another strange look as he headed to the bathroom.

Cathy put her cup in the sink and walked to the front door. She wanted to have a look at the backyard in case Michael Potter had left a sign of

143

his visit. If he had, she wanted to have an explanation ready in case the kids noticed. She took the key from the screen door and locked the house from the outside before she went downstairs. She was going to take no risks. She stood on the porch for a couple of minutes looking across the road, but there was no sign of life at the caravan park. Hurrying down the steps, she quickly opened the unlocked gate and went into the backyard. The postholes that Joe had dug for the deck looked the same, but a small pile of dirt a third of the way along the new fence caught her attention. A new hole had been dug and half-filled in. Joe's shovel which was usually with the rest of the tools at the back of the house was lying abandoned near the fence.

Cathy picked it up and took it over and put it against the back of the house. The kids wouldn't notice the hole. She'd try to think of a way to explain it to Grant and Ryan if they asked.

Hurrying back upstairs, she unlocked the screen door, her eyes flicking over to the caravan park again.

'Are you pair ready, yet?' she called.

By the time Cathy got back to the house after dropping the kids at the school gates, Grant's RAM was parked outside. She left her car on the road to give them better access down the side and walked quietly into the backyard.

Her heart plummeted. Grant was standing next to the newly dug hole with a strange expression on his face as he stared down at the disturbed earth.

'Morning, Grant,' she called out.

He jumped and turned to face her. 'Hello, Cathy. Did you have more trouble last night?'

'Trouble?' She raised her eyebrows as she walked over to him, and kept her voice as level as she was able to. 'What do you mean?'

'Someone's dug a hole here.'

'Oh, that.' She waved one hand dismissively. 'I was helping Billy with his homework.'

'By digging a three-foot hole?'

'Um, yes. Soil science.'

Grant looked at her suspiciously and then appeared to accept her explanation. 'More interesting than when I was at high school.'

'Okay, I'll leave you to it,' she said. 'I have some chores to do.'

She knew he was watching her as she walked away. He still hadn't mentioned that he'd been at Bindarra Creek High School. Grant Cummings was up to something.

He'd looked clearly unimpressed that

someone had been digging in the yard.

***

The first thing that Grant had noticed when he walked onsite was a disturbance in the ground in the exact place he'd been looking at. When he'd measured it out from Sally's instructions the other day, he'd taken good notice of where it was. Someone else obviously knew, and they'd beaten him to it.

He could tell Sally there was nothing to be found because if there had been, it was gone now.

He wondered if it was Cathy who'd dug the hole. If she was innocent, she too would have been surprised by the digging, but she had come up with the homework story, so he knew she was lying.

Grant stood there and stared, and then realised that Cathy could see him from the kitchen window. As he moved across to his toolbox to get his measuring tape, he thought about what he knew.

He'd put money on it being Michael Potter. Maybe he and Cathy had gotten together and compared what each of them knew. But that didn't make sense with her being so scared the night before last.

A ute came down the drive, Ryan driving and Joe in the passenger seat. Grant watched as Ryan parked near the gate and they both climbed out. A pump sat on the back tray, and he walked over to help them.

'Morning,' he called out. 'Want a hand to get that off?'

'Yes, please,' Ryan replied. 'It's heavier than it looks.'

Once it was offloaded, Ryan removed an extension cord from the back of his ute. 'I'll get Cathy to open up the back door and plug it in.' He glanced at the hole near the fence. 'What are you digging there?'

'Not me. Cathy said Billy was out here digging.'

Ryan frowned. 'I hope he hasn't touched the footings.'

Joe wandered over to the house and looked in each hole. 'All good. What are you working on today, Grant?' he asked as Ryan disappeared up the side of the house.

'I'm going to measure up for the garden boxes and the new chook shed, and then I'll probably go to Tamworth to get the timber. Unless you guys need a hand?' He'd see Sally while he was there and tell her to forget all her grand schemes. Maybe she'd try to get a job, but he doubted it.

'We'll be right. Once we get the water out of the holes, it'll be pretty easy to finish the footings. Ryan's booked the concrete delivery for tomorrow.'

'Okay, I'll get to work then.'

Cathy came back outside with Ryan. 'I'm sorry,' she said looking at Joe and Ryan, her voice shaking. 'I'll tell Billy no more digging. Please don't say anything to him, he'll be upset.'

Grant frowned as he looked at Cathy. Her face was white; he hadn't noticed the shadows beneath her eyes when she'd been out here before. He'd been too busy looking at the disturbed ground.

'Not a problem, Cathy,' Ryan said. 'I wasn't having a go. Just make sure he stays away from the footings.'

'Promise you won't say anything to him though.' Cathy's hands were clenched tightly in front of her.

Ryan looked at her curiously. 'Not a word.'

'I'm sorry. I should've told you Billy was mucking around out here yesterday afternoon. I told him not to do anything but it looks like he's done something. I'll have a word to him. I won't let the kids down here again till you've finished the deck.'

'I thought it was homework and you were helping him,' Grant said. Cathy was lying through her teeth. Her eyes widened. Something had happened here; she looked terrified.

Cathy wasn't a good liar. She needed to learn if you were telling the truth you needed to get your story straight; Grant knew that better than anyone.

'Yes, it was homework.' Her voice was terse. 'I have to go and hang the washing out.' She almost ran up the side of the house.

Ryan looked at Grant. 'What was all that about?'

Grant shrugged. 'I must have misunderstood her before you arrived. Come on, let's get this pump over there.'

As they wheeled the pump over to the back of the house, Cathy came back around, a basket of washing under her arm. She placed it near the gate and walked over to Ryan.

'I've been thinking,' she said.

'That's a dangerous occupation,' Joe said, but there was no answering smile from Cathy.

'What's up, Cath?' Ryan asked.

'Listen, seeing it's so wet out here and you've got the fence done, I'm not in any hurry for the deck at all. I'm sure you've got other jobs to do, Ryan. What do you think? Why not just leave mine for a few weeks and let the ground dry out? We're fine with the backyard fence finished now and I can probably think about getting a dog for Billy.' Her words spilled over each other as she spoke quickly.

'If you get a dog for Billy, it could still just get out underneath the house,' Grant pointed out. 'We need to close in under the deck if you want that.'

'Silly me,' she said. 'Okay, maybe no dog yet.'

'I could easily put a low barrier from the gate and under the house across to the other side fence. Would you like me to do that?' Grant frowned as he noticed the sheen of perspiration on her forehead. It was only early and the temperature was quite mild.

'Could you do it today? I've sort of heard about a rescue dog that would be good. If you could do it today, I can get the dog tomorrow. I can pay extra for the rush job.'

Ryan frowned and glanced at Grant and then Joe.

Grant raised his eyebrows. 'I can do that fence today,' he said. 'I've got enough fencing material in my shed. Ryan and Joe don't need to help. They can do what they have to.'

Cathy put her hands on her hips. 'This might sound a bit silly, but I've been thinking about this deck; it was all Lea's idea. I don't even know if I need it. Let me think about it some more. Okay?'

Ryan spoke slowly. 'We'll pump out today, Cathy. Lea's already paid a deposit for the deck, and I've bought all the materials.'

'Oh.' Cathy chewed on her lip, and as she lifted her hand to push her hair back, Grant noticed how much she was shaking.

'I've still got the garden boxes to do, but I'll be finished in a couple of days,' he said.

Cathy waved her other hand. 'I'm happy to pay for them, but we don't need them just yet. If you guys have other things to do, please just go and do those jobs. We're fine here.'

'Fine?' Ryan walked over to stand beside Cathy. 'That's a funny thing to say. Are you okay, Cath? You're a bit pale. You're not coming down with something, are you?'

'I'm fine. I like my own company and I might sound rude, but if I haven't got you guys here in the yard all the time, it'll give me a chance to settle in more easily.'

Ryan nodded. 'Okay. I guess if that's what you want. I've paid for the pump and the concrete's been ordered, so we'll spend today and tomorrow here, and then give you a bit of a break.'

Cathy nodded and stumbled as she walked back to the gate.

'Something's very wrong,' Ryan said quietly. 'That is totally not Cathy.'

'I wondered too,' Grant said. 'She was talking about soil homework and Billy, and then she was really adamant that we didn't talk to him. She obviously forgot what she told me only half an hour ago. I think someone's been in here and I have a fair idea who it was.'

'Mike Potter?' Ryan asked.

Grant nodded. 'I suspect it could be.'

'What's he after? I know he's been in jail, but I don't know why. I think she needs to get to the police station. I know she and Jac tried the other day and left a message.'

'Riley's been really busy,' Joe said. 'I've met him at the pub a couple of times. And some of the others are on leave.'

'Riley?' Grant asked.

'Riley Morgan. The senior sergeant. What do you reckon we should do?' Joe asked.

'Let's just get to work for the morning, and let the day pass normally, and see if Cathy settles a bit. She might open up eventually,' Grant suggested.

'I'll give Jaclyn a ring.' Ryan glanced at Grant. 'She might come into town and see her. Find out what's wrong.'

'Sounds like a plan,' Grant said. 'I'll have a think about what I'll do.'

'Any ideas?' Ryan asked.

'No, but leave it with me. I'll fill you in later.'

Grant began measuring up for the garden boxes, but his focus wasn't on it. He'd googled Michael Potter after he'd got nothing out of him. He had a criminal record that went back from the time he was at high school. Petty theft, sexual assault, and a string of serious offences. According to the court reports, he'd spent more time in jail than out. Grant knew exactly when that had started; he'd just gotten away in time. Leaving Bindarra Creek when he was seventeen was the most sensible decision he'd made in his life; even though his parents had been disappointed when he'd left school and town.

'Damn.' He cursed as he finished measuring the area for the next garden box. The first measurements had completely gone out of his head. It had nothing to do with the noise of the pump over near the house; it was more the thoughts in his head that were interfering with his concentration.

His anger built as he wondered how Mick Potter had frightened Cathy so much. He wouldn't put anything past that lowlife.

Even before this had happened, he'd spent way too much time thinking about Cathy. She was a good person in a difficult situation. He admired her, and he tried to tell himself it had nothing to do with the physical attraction that kicked in every time he was with her. He'd only known her a few days, but she had touched him in a different way. He couldn't stop thinking about her, and couldn't wait to get back here every day.

As if he'd conjured her up, she reappeared with the same basket of washing she'd had under her arm before. The clothesline was near the gate and she put the basket on the ground and began to hang the washing out. Usually in jeans, she was wearing a dress now and it swirled around her slim legs in the light breeze. Her hair was damp; it looked like she'd taken a shower since she was out here before, and her face had more colour than it had when she was speaking to them earlier.

She looked up and saw him looking at her, and smiled; even though it had been a fleeting smile, it made him feel good. It was all he could do not to walk over and stand near her.

Grant went back to his measuring and tried to keep his head down. After a couple of minutes, he was surrounded by a sweet fragrance and he looked up. Cathy was standing close watching him. Her expression was guarded.

'Grant?'

'Yes, Cathy?' He put everything he could into the smile he gave her, and was surprised to see her pale cheeks go pink.

'I'm sorry I was so rude before. And you probably think I'm going silly with all the crap I was saying. I'd . . . I'd just had some news that upset me, and I was very preoccupied. I'm sorry.'

Grant couldn't help himself. He reached out and took her hand and was pleased when she stepped towards him willingly. 'I know you were upset, and I want to help you. Can you tell me what your news was?'

She opened her mouth as she held his eyes, and then looked away and shook her head. 'No, I can't.'

'Is it to do with Mike Potter?'

Her eyes widened and her hand gripped his fingers tightly.

Before he could keep her talking, the pump switched off and the silence was sweet after the racket it had been making as he'd worked.

'Cathy? I can help you.' She shook her head, and he was taken back when her eyes filled with tears. 'Please let me.'

'No one can help me. I can't tell you—'

'Holy hell!'

They turned as one as Joe yelled out and stepped back from where he was digging.

Ryan was standing near the pump. 'What's wrong? Have you hurt yourself?'

As they watched, Ryan hurried over to Joe and his brother grabbed his arm and pulled him over to the hole where he'd been digging.

Ryan leaned over and peered down. He took a sudden step back and looked at Joe and shook his head. Grant's heart sank.

What had they found?

Surely what Mike Potter had told Sally

155

hadn't been true?

If he had been telling the truth and had come looking, maybe he hadn't found what he was looking for because of the water in the holes. Although the hole that both Ryan and Joe were looking down at again was nowhere near the place where Grant had figured out it was, and where the hole had been dug yesterday.

He looked down realising that Cathy was still gripping his fingers.

'What is it?' she asked with a frown. 'What have they found?'

'Come on, let's go see.' He was pleased when Cathy kept her hand in his; it seemed to strengthen her confidence. As they got closer, Ryan put up his hand to stop them.

'Stay there, Cathy,' he said, distress clouding his face.

She picked up on it immediately as Grant had.

'What is it, what's wrong?' Her voice shook as though she knew what they had found.

Maybe she did, Grant thought. Maybe he was giving Cathy too much credit for being the injured party here. He let go of her hand. 'You stay here, I'll go see.'

'There's something in the hole.' Ryan looked up and held Grant's gaze.

'What is it?' Cathy repeated. 'What have you found?'

Grant expected Ryan to say that it was a metal box or similar because he'd heard the shovel hit it yesterday. It certainly wasn't something soft that money could have been buried in.

Ryan spoke slowly. 'We'll have to call the police,' he said.

Cathy let out a guttural cry and Grant took her hand again; he couldn't help himself.

'It's okay, Cathy, calm down.' He stroked her fingers trying to soothe her distress but she jerked in his grip.

'No!' Her cry was shrill, just short of a scream. 'No police. Please we can't have the police here. If you must, let me go and get Billy and Josie. We have to hide. I have to take them away from here. Keep them safe. Show me what it is.'

Her fingers curled around his, seeking comfort again. It shouldn't feel so good.

'Come on. We'll find out exactly what's going on here.' Grant led her closer to the hole.

Ryan shook his head. 'Maybe you should just wait, Cathy.'

Grant stepped forward and looked into the hole. The earth was dark brown with a reddish tinge, shining from the water seeping down the sides. He leaned further and his attention was caught by the bright light shining on something. He peered down and it took a moment before he realised what he was seeing. His stomach dropped and he took a step back.

Cathy was standing behind him and she pushed herself forward. 'I want to see.'

Ryan tried to stop her, but she leaned over next to Grant and her long drawn-out keening cry sent goosebumps down Grant's spine as Cathy looked at the human skull.

Grant spun around swiftly as her body crumpled and she teetered over the wide hole.

'Oh my God,' she whispered. 'It's Russ. Don't let the children see. Please don't let them see.'

Grant supported Cathy until he regained his balance, his arms holding her close before he half bent and lifted her. Her head lolled to the side, and her eyes were closed. Ryan and Joe walked beside him as he carried Cathy around to the front steps.

'I'll get the door,' Joe said.

'Ryan, before you call the police, I think you need to call an ambulance.'

Chapter 15

Cathy was aware of the softness beneath her head and back, and she moaned as she tried to open her eyes. The last thing she remembered was carrying the washing basket out.

'How did I get into my bed?' she murmured, her mouth dry.

Maybe it was all a dream?

'It's okay, Cathy.' Grant's voice confused her.

Why is he in my bedroom?

'Just take it easy, you fainted. Can you hear me?'

She finally managed to open her eyes. Grant was sitting on the edge of her bed, looking down at her.

'Good, you're back with us.' He half turned and she noticed Joe standing near the door. 'Can you get Cathy a drink from the kitchen please, mate?'

Cathy's vision was still blurry and she closed her eyes again. 'I'm okay. I just feel a bit sick.'

'Just lie there. The paramedics will be here in a minute.'

All of a sudden everything came rushing back, and she cried out. 'No. I'm okay.' She struggled to sit up. 'The police can't come. Please don't let them be seen here.'

Grant's voice was calm and even. 'Cathy, they have to. I know you saw what was in the hole. It has to be reported and the house will be a crime scene until they do a forensic investigation.'

'Please help me sit up, Grant. I feel better. I won't faint again. It was just the shock, and I don't need the paramedics.'

As she spoke, Ryan appeared in her doorway. 'They're out of town anyway, there's been an accident on the Boggabri Road. The operator said to take you down to the hospital.'

Cathy shook her head, and the room didn't spin. 'I'm okay. I don't need to see anyone. Like I told Grant, it was just the shock. I didn't get any sleep last night, and I've had a lot on my mind today. Seeing that . . . seeing that in the ground pushed me over the edge. I'll be okay.'

An icy calm descended on Cathy as she considered all the possibilities. With a deep exhalation, she swung her legs over the side of the bed, narrowly missing Grant.

'I know the police will have to be called. Have you called them yet, Ryan?'

'No, we were making sure you were okay

before we did anything.'

Joe came in with a glass of water, and she took it gratefully. 'Thank you.' She didn't speak again until she'd drained it.

'I need to go to school, and I need to get Josie and Billy. I want them with me so I know they're safe.'

She intercepted the look between Ryan and Grant.

Grant stood and looked down at her. 'I'll drive you. You know you won't be able to stay here, don't you? It will be a crime scene.'

'I understand that.'

'How about we leave the kids until school finishes, and we get you sorted? You'll have to pack up what you need, for you and the kids,' Grant said.

As Ryan came over and stood beside Grant, Cathy pushed herself to her feet. 'And Cath, you don't want them here. You know what Billy's like. He'll twig right away that something is wrong.'

'Especially once the police get here,' Grant added. 'Although that might be a while because I'm sure they'll come from Tamworth.'

'And all the locals are out at the accident,' Joe said. 'Apparently, there was a fatality.'

'Oh no. Not a local, please. Although any death is awful. So, it will be a few hours before there's any sign of police here, you think?' Cathy's tension eased a little. All she could think of was Michael Potter seeing the police car and going straight to the school to take Josie. 'Do you think so?'

'Look, Cathy.' Grant seemed to have taken charge. 'We can delay ringing them for a little while until you feel comfortable. We can help you get sorted and then call them, and then collect the kids.'

Cathy put her hand to her face and closed her eyes. 'Where will we go? I'm not going back to the farm. It wouldn't be fair to Cleo and Jon.'

'You're welcome to come out to our place,' Ryan offered.

'No. But thank you. I'll find somewhere in town. I'm not going to rely on people's hospitality anymore.'

'It's called friendship, Cathy,' Ryan said quietly. 'I know Jac will want you there.'

'No, I have to be in town. I need to start looking for a job. I'll find somewhere to rent.'

'Are you sure?' Grant asked.

'Yes.'

'In that case, I'm happy to offer the empty apartment next to mine. I haven't rented it out yet.'

Cathy thought for a minute. Grant had been helpful and kind to her but she needed to know if she could trust him.

'Okay, but will you answer one question for

me? Why are you pretending you don't know me? I know you went to school here, but you seem to be very secretive. I want to know why.'

'I didn't know if you'd remember me or not. I was only at high school with you a year or so. I guess when I came back here, I'd forgotten what long memories small towns have.' He held her gaze as she looked up at him. 'I did have my reasons for coming here, and I'll tell you later, but for the time being, you have my word you can trust me. I'm not here to hurt anyone, but I did come here to find something out. I came to River Cottage looking for something, but I didn't get a chance to look.'

'Does it have something to do with Michael Potter and . . . and Russ?'

'Yes.'

Chapter 16

Later that night, Cathy and Grant sat opposite each other at a table on his back verandah. Josie and Billy had accepted the move with little explanation, being told that there were some structural issues with the cottage and they had to move out for a while.

Grant was surprised by their acceptance and realised how little these two children had. As long as Josie knew her books were at the new place, and Billy had his cricket gear, they were happy. It hadn't taken them long to move what Cathy had packed and take it to the apartment on the other side of his duplex.

Ryan and Joe had helped and carted boxes to the two utes, and Cathy had unpacked everything before school was finished for the day. Even Red the rooster was loaded in a crate and was now scratching around the small garden behind the two apartments.

Grant nursed a beer, but Cathy had opted for a cup of tea once she'd checked the kids were settled and asleep.

By the time Riley Morgan and the senior constable had arrived at the cottage, Cathy had picked the kids up and they were all at the apartment. Ryan and Grant had filled the senior sergeant in and he'd locked the gate and the constable had placed police tape across the front driveway.

'The Tamworth detectives and forensics will be here about nine tomorrow,' Riley said. 'They'll want to talk to Cathy, and we'll need to interview her in-laws too. Until we know how old the bones are, and what sex, it's going to be tough for the family.' The unspoken thought in everyone's minds was the disappearance of Russ Kendall.

Grant had kept quiet, but he knew he'd have a lot to say tomorrow when the detectives arrived. That was going to be hard, but not as tough as the talk he was about to have with Cathy.

He'd promised honesty, and even though what he had to tell her was going to be hard, she had to know.

They were both quiet as they sat there. The last of the light was fading quickly. Grant loved the long dusk of spring in the bush.

Cathy broke the silence. 'Did you have dinner, Grant? I didn't think to offer you any when I cooked for the kids. With all the work and moving you did, you wouldn't have had time to cook.'

'Cook?' He smiled at her. There was more colour in her face than there had been all day, and she was still wearing that pretty dress she'd had on since this morning. 'Most of my cooking is done by Thea Levonis. She makes a mean hamburger.'

'You ate out? I could have sent a plate over.'

'I eat out six nights out of seven. Either the Cyprus Café or the Riverside Pub.'

'That's terrible. The least I can do to make up for all your help is cook a meal and send it over every night. And speaking of that, you need to tell me how to sort out the rent. How much and where I pay it.'

Grant shook his head. 'We've got enough to talk about tonight without worrying about that. The place was going to stay empty for a while anyway. Until I decided what I was going to do.'

'What do you mean do?'

'Until I decided if I'd stay in Bindarra Creek or not. I didn't know how it would be after all these years, but I feel comfortable here.' He held her eyes and the colour in her face deepened.

'It's that sort of town, isn't it?' she finally said when she looked up again. 'It sort of wraps itself around you. People care about each other but still give each other privacy.'

'They do. I've enjoyed the time here, even with everything that's been going on.' Grant couldn't help himself. He reached over and took her hand. 'I hope you don't judge me by what I'm about to tell you. I enjoy spending time with you, Cathy.

166

And after this is all over, I thought we could maybe go out for dinner one night.'

'I'm happy to cook for you,' she said.

'I know you are, but I mean, like a date. You know with babysitters for the kids. Maybe we could drive into Tamworth if you worry about local gossip.'

If it was possible, the pink in her cheeks was even brighter. She lifted her eyes and held his steadily. 'I would like that very much. And I'm going to have to get used to gossip once the town hears about the bones under River Cottage.'

'I wanted to ask you that before I told you the truth. It's going to be hard, but let me tell you everything before you ask questions. Or even worse take off back to your apartment.'

'I'm listening.' Cathy squeezed his fingers gently and left her hand in his.

Grant smoothed his thumb over the top of her soft skin. 'There are two parts to this story and they both involve Russ. I'll start with the most recent and you have to remember this is all hearsay. I'd left town before it happened. Actually, I'd left town before both.'

'Tell me, Grant,' she said quietly.

'I don't know if you remember the robbery at the Riverside Pub about fifteen years ago?'

'I do, it was the weekend after Russ dropped

me. It was the talk of Bindarra Creek, and the talk at school.'

'And what about when Russ disappeared? Do you remember anything strange about that time?'

'Nothing really strange. I knew he was having a boys' night with Michael Potter and a couple of others. That's why I went out to Lea and David's farm that weekend. We used to go out a couple of times a month so the kids could visit them. Billy loved the animals out there. I think Lea knew I was doing it tough too. She'd always send us home with an esky full of meat and would slip a hundred dollars to me for groceries. After that weekend, I never saw Russ again, and it sounds dreadful, but I was absolutely relieved that he'd taken off. He was a cruel man, and he hurt me a few times. Especially when he'd been drinking. That was one of the reasons I didn't want to come back to the cottage. I think it was why I was so difficult about everything Lea wanted to do there for me. It holds some pretty nasty memories, and now, even more.'

Grant cleared his throat. 'It was Russ and Mike Potter who took the pub takings that night.'

'Are you sure? The police always reckoned it was the barmaid. She was an English backpacker and she left town that night.'

'It's the truth. That came from Mike Potter to my sister. He wrote to her when he was in jail. And I know it's true because I was supposed to be with them that night. I left school and town the next weekend. I didn't want to be associated with Russ and Mike, so I talked my parents into letting me leave town. I moved to Melbourne to live with my aunt and finish my schooling there. It made a huge difference in my life. Mike told Sally that they buried the money in the backyard of River Cottage, because no one lived there. They deliberately left it so there was no sign of them having sudden money. As far as Mike knows, it was still there when Russ disappeared.'

Cathy shivered. 'He is one scary man. I feel much safer here, with you next door. I think Josie will settle a lot more too. I won't move back to River Cottage. Not when they've found those bones. I couldn't live there, knowing that. And it wouldn't be fair to the kids. I also worry that it could be Russ.' Cathy took her hand from his and put it over her mouth. 'Oh my God, what if it is Russ, and they think I killed him? I never thought of that.'

'I'm sure you'll be interviewed, but just for them to get information.'

Her eyes widened. 'Or what if Michael Potter killed him and buried him there one weekend when we were out at the farm? I'm sure he'd be capable of it.'

'Leave the supposition and investigation to the police, Cathy.' Grant smiled when she lowered her hand, and it crept back into his.

'What was the second thing you had to tell me?'

He took a deep breath. 'Mike wrote to Sally from prison and asked her to look for the money. He told her exactly where it was buried. That's why I took the job from Lea, Cathy. I came back to Bindarra to look for that money for my sister. Mainly to show her she was wrong; I really didn't believe what he told her was true. Can you forgive me for the deception?'

There was a long silence before Cathy answered. 'There's been a lot of deception over the years. Why was Sally so interested in the money?'

'This one is going to hurt, and it's going to impact on Billy and Josie, depending on what you want to do.'

'Sally—'

'Hang on?' she said. 'Sally Cummings is your sister?'

'Yes. Sally lives in Tamworth—'

'I can't believe it. I was forever grateful to her because Russ dropped me for her. I was trying to get away from him, but he was really possessive and Russ always called the shots. He was the one who broke it off and I was so relieved. I was only in Year 8. I should have stayed away from him four years later, but one night of too many drinks, and I fell pregnant with Billy.'

'I remember you at school when Russ got his tentacles around you. You were a quiet, shy little thing, and I knew what he was up to. He always went for the good girls, and he held an attraction for them. He was very charismatic and he sucked me into his group too, until I woke up to him. Just in time. He wanted me to go to the pub with them that night.'

'Why would Michael have told Sally about the money though?' Cathy tipped her head to the side and Grant knew this was the bit that could break their relationship before it even began. 'I don't understand. Were they friends too?'

'No, but Mick knew he could tempt Sally with the money.' Grant ran his free hand through his hair. 'Russ Kendall ruined her life, but she also needs to take some responsibility for the way she'd handled how things turned out. She's lost her moral compass and Sally was quite happy to take a share of the money if it was there.'

'How did he ruin her life?' Cathy asked very quietly. She was still and her hand tensed in his.

'Sally fell pregnant the year after I left. They

were both in Year 12. He wanted nothing to do with her, and he claimed that she'd been sleeping around. She swears he was the only one, but he threatened her if she didn't get rid of it, he'd badmouth her all around town.'

'Russ was good at that. Blackmail, I mean,' Cathy said bleakly. 'And the baby? Did she have it or—'

'Mum and Dad supported Sally. They moved to Melbourne, and I went back to live with them while I finished Year 12 and a horticulture degree at uni.' Grant touched her face until she looked at him. 'Cathy, my nephew Beau is seventeen.'

'And a half-brother to Billy and Josie. Oh, God. What a mess.'

'It is.'

Cathy's hand was still in his, but her eyes filled with tears as she stared at him. He waited until she spoke, unsure of what she was thinking.

Her voice broke, and she dropped his hand and rose to her feet. 'Grant, would you hold me?'

Grant was on his feet in a flash, walked around the small table and took her in his arms. Cathy rested her head on his shoulder and leaned into him. Her body was soft, and as he held her he could feel the fineness of her frame. Holding her filled a need within him. She lifted her head and looked up at him. 'Sometimes it just all gets too much, and now this.' Her cheeks were pink and her lips slightly open. He moved and rested the palm of one hand against her cheek. It was wet with tears. 'He's hurt so many people. His parents, your sister, the kids have never known a father.'

'And you have no idea where he is?' Grant asked quietly.

'I haven't seen Russ since the day I left to go to the farm when Billy was two and Josie was three months old. The police theory was that he drowned in the Akuna River, but it was drought and the river was barely flowing. My theory was he wanted to disappear, but I guess if the money was still there, he might be dead. He would have come back to get it. It was over two hundred thousand dollars, the police said. The pokie takings for a week, and the pub cash. Michael Potter said he had a new woman and there was no fear of him coming back. I've always been scared he would, and the kids would see what sort of man their father was.' Her body trembled as she sighed. 'In one way it would be closure if it is his body at River Cottage.'

'The money could still be there.'

'No. I watched Michael carry a bag out from the backyard the other night. Where the soil was disturbed, when I told you all those lies about Billy and his homework. I googled it; that much money

173

would weigh less than forty kilos, but I wondered if it would still be okay.'

'If it was wrapped in plastic, it would be. You always see those sorts of things on the news,' Grant said. 'So, it looks like he got it after all. You haven't told the police any of this, have you?'

No, and I don't know what to do. He said he'd come back and take Josie. That's why the police can't be involved.'

'Cathy. It's too late for that now. There's a body in your yard, and you know he's got the proceeds of that crime. For all you know, he could be going to meet Russ. The police need to know. You have to talk to them. Tonight. He's already got a head start if he's left town, and if he's watching your place still, he'll see the police tape. He could know about the body. Hell, he might have even put it there.'

'There are so many things that it could be, aren't there? If I talk to the police, will you help me protect Billy and Josie? I'm scared they're going to arrest me.'

'Of course, I will, sweetheart.' The endearment came naturally. 'And I'll look after you too. You're not going to get arrested. We'll call Riley Morgan now and get him to come here.'

Cathy nodded. 'One thing first before it all goes to hell.'

'What's that?' he asked.

'Would you mind terribly much if I kissed you?'

A smile broke slowly over Grant's face, and he held her close. He lowered his head and Cathy sighed as he slid his mouth gently across her cheek. He teased the corner of her lips with his, and she turned her head slightly so that her lips clung to his, as though she was reluctant for their first kiss to end.

If Grant had his way, it would be the first of many.

They stood like that for a long time, until she pulled away.

'Come on,' she said. 'It's time we called Riley Morgan.'

Several times over the next long hours, Grant closed his eyes, still able to feel the soft warmth of Cathy's lips beneath his.

Chapter 17

'I apologise that we didn't get back to you yesterday about the intruder the night before.'

Cathy nodded. 'That's okay.'

Senior Sergeant Riley Morgan conducted the interview in a professional manner. His questions were probing, and Cathy had to hold back tears as she took him over the events of the past fifteen years. Having worked away from Bindarra Creek in Sydney as an undercover cop for eight years of that time, he was au fait with some of the case. More pertinent, he'd been a year below Russ and Michael at school, so was well aware of the personalities involved.

'And you've had no contact with Russ since before the weekend he went missing?' he asked Cathy as they sat at the dining room table in Grant's apartment. Cathy went next door and checked on the kids every fifteen minutes. The doors and windows were all locked, and she had the air conditioning running to keep the unit cool.

She stood looking down at each of her children. It was only a two-bedroom unit and Billy's only complaint was that he had to share a room with his little sister. They were both fast asleep and, for the millionth time, she gave thanks that both Billy and Josie favoured her in looks. Neither of them looked the slightest bit like their father, nor had they shown any of his traits so far. She wondered what the other boy was like. If he was anything like Russ, she would do all she could to keep him away from her pair.

Grant had told her he might be giving him a job in Bindarra Creek, and she still had to process how she felt about that. It wasn't the boy's fault.

'That's right.' She closed her eyes as she answered Senior Sergeant Morgan. 'I cooked dinner on Thursday night, and he went out shearing the next morning. He always went out for a drink after work, and sometimes he stayed out all night, so I didn't worry when he wasn't at the cottage when I went out to the farm on Saturday morning.'

'And he was shearing out towards Boggabri?'

'I don't know. He never told me where he was working.'

'And how would you describe your relationship with him. You never married, did you? It was a defacto relationship?'

'Yes, it was, but Russ insisted I took his name.'

'How did you feel when he didn't come back? Were you happy, Cathy?'

A quiver of unease ran through Cathy. She

knew she had nothing to do with Russ's disappearance, or maybe even his death.

She frowned and glanced at Grant. 'Should I answer questions like that? Should I have a solicitor, or a lawyer, or whatever they're called? In case the police think I killed him because he was violent to me?'

'You're not being charged with anything, Cathy,' Riley said gently. 'We're just trying to get a clear picture of what happened when he left. To ease your mind a little, we doubt very much that it is Russell Kendall as he was arrested in Western Australia earlier this year. But if you want representation, that's your prerogative.'

'Arrested? Is he still in jail?'

'He is on bail, but under strict conditions. I was speaking to the police over there earlier.'

'What did he do? Did he hurt someone?' Cathy whispered. 'Wouldn't it have been in the paper if he was arrested? I google his name every few weeks. You can check my phone history, can't you? You can search my internet history. If I'd killed him, I wouldn't be googling him, would I?'

'Can Cathy take a break now? You can see this is upsetting her.'

'Just a couple more things and I'll leave you in peace. Are you happy to answer my questions?'

'Yes, let's get it over with,' she said.

178

'Thank you. How did you feel when he didn't come back? Were you happy, Cathy?'

'I was happy when he disappeared, but I wanted him to have left, not drowned. I wouldn't wish that on anyone.' She lifted her chin. 'I don't know what state of mind he was in. He was always angry with me. We never talked about anything,' Cathy said. 'Those two years living with Russ were hell.'

'Thank you. I wanted to know so I knew whether to tell you that Russell is very much alive. He changed his name, but his identity came to light recently when he was fingerprinted for a bank robbery in Perth. His profile was on the police database in New South Wales, and the connection was made.'

Cathy shook her head. 'Poor Lea and David. They are going to be devastated all over again. Should I call them?' Her voice broke. 'And how am I going to tell my children one day that their father is a criminal? I'll take them away from Bindarra Creek. The history here is too much, and this will be the talk of the town.'

The senior sergeant gave her a few minutes to compose herself. 'As the owners of River Cottage, Lea and David Kendall have been contacted about the finding of the human remains.'

'Okay. Thank you. Do they know where I

am? Don't worry. I'll call them in the morning.'

The senior sergeant nodded. 'Cathy, a couple of detectives from Tamworth will be here tomorrow, and I'll pass on your report, but they may still want to interview you. I've just got a few more questions, particularly about Michael Potter.'

'Okay.'

'Tell me exactly when you saw him and try to recall exactly what he said on the occasion he came to your door.'

Cathy's voice trembled as she went through the events of last night.

'And you didn't think to call the police?' Riley asked when she had finished.

'No, I was terrified for my children. Have you seen him lately? He's a huge thug of a man now, and he said he'd come back and take Josie if I so much as breathed a word to anyone.'

Grant reached for her hand and intervened. 'When Ryan and Joe Rossiter, and I, arrived at Cathy's place this morning to work, we knew there was something wrong. She wasn't herself, and just about insisted we leave.'

'I was scared I'd crack and tell you what happened if you all stayed. You were all so kind to me. And then Joe hit that skull with the spade and I went to pieces. All I could think of was Josie's fear when he stared at her through the window. His teeth are filed to points. He's absolutely terrifying to look at and my ten-year-old will have to live with that.'

'Cathy, to set your mind at rest, I can tell you that Michael Potter is under police guard in the local hospital, but I ask that both you and Grant keep that to yourselves.'

'In hospital?' Cathy's mouth dropped open. 'What happened?'

'He was involved in the accident out on the Boggabri Road this morning. That's one of the reasons we didn't get back to you today. There were two fatalities, and Potter is in a serious condition.'

'Are you sure he can't get away?'

'There are two policemen at his door at all times, so be reassured.'

'Don't trust him. Please.'

'He is secure, Cathy.'

Senior Sergeant Morgan stood. 'That's the interview over, Cathy. I'd like to express my personal regret that you've gone through this, both today and over the past years. I know Lea and David have supported you above and beyond, and I hope the local community has too.'

'Thank you, Riley. I appreciate it. Bindarra Creek people have been very kind to me. I think I've been too much of a recluse, but all that's going to change now.' She looked up at Grant and smiled.

'Just one more thing to be aware of, Cathy,'

Riley said as she reached the door. 'Forensic examination is a slow process. It could be a few weeks before we know what's been found in the yard of River Cottage. Maybe months. So don't plan on going back there for a while.'

'Riley, I'm not planning on moving back there at all.'

He nodded and opened the door. 'I'll see you both in the morning.'

Chapter 18

Saying good night to Cathy was sweet, but brief. She was anxious to get next door and be with her children. Grant kissed her goodnight at her door and waited until he heard the chain go up before he went back to his unit, a smile on his face.

How could his life have changed so quickly? Meeting Cathy, even in such dreadful circumstances had renewed his faith in the possibility of happiness. He was grateful that she hadn't judged him for his deception, and she had made the first move.

He would have held back and wasted time. Now, with them being open and honest with each other, he could support her. He'd been tempted to offer to sleep on the sofa in her unit but had held back so she didn't think he was being too forward, but he knew how nervous she was about bloody Michael Potter.

He was close enough that he would hear anything out of the ordinary. The best part was the police station was across the road. He'd looked out there before he'd come inside. The station was ablaze with light; he guessed that there'd be someone there all night. That should reassure Cathy too.

He needed to call Sally and hoped that she'd

be in a better frame of mind, knowing that Michael was in custody, and that Russ was alive. Grant frowned as he remembered Riley had asked them to keep some of it to themselves.

He wouldn't say anything specific; he'd just touch base with Sally and see how she was.

He picked up his phone and dialled her number, but his attention was taken by a noise outside as he waited for his sister to pick up. Someone had kicked a garbage bin of bottles over in the street. It was recycling night, and all the bins were out.

Grant moved across to the window and peered through the vertical blind, but there was no sign of any activity out there or evidence of a bin knocked over. With a shrug, he let the blind drop as Sally picked up the call.

'Hello, Grant. Any news?'

'Not yet. I'm just calling to see how you and Beau are.'

'We're actually good. There's a new youth worker at the school, and Beau thinks he's pretty cool. "Sick" was the term he used, but I think that means good these days.'

Grant chuckled. 'I think it might too. You sound good too, Sal.'

'When Beau's happy, I'm happy. This Chris guy is even helping me get his building traineeship application done. I think we might have turned a corner, Grant.'

'That's great news.'

She sighed. 'I'm sorry I was so pushy with that Mick Potter stuff. I was just clutching at straws. You'll probably be pleased to hear I've picked up some hours at the R.S.L club in the bistro. If he contacts me again, I'll tell him to take a hike.'

'That's a good plan.' Grant would have loved to be able to tell her that Mick Potter wouldn't be contacting anyone—except his lawyer—for quite a while. But he'd be able to fill her in later.

When Cathy was comfortable with the idea, he'd take her and the kids to Tamworth to meet Sally and Beau.

If she was ever comfortable with the idea, that was. He wouldn't ever push; that was entirely her call.

'I'll be over in Tamworth in the next few days. I'll call in.'

'I'd like that. And, Grant, I want you to know I do appreciate you. What you agreed to do for me at that house was above and beyond.'

Grant didn't comment. It was only a matter of time before Sally heard the news. He'd keep an eye on the media and call her again as soon as the discovery of the bones, and Potter's arrest were made public.

'Okay say hello—hang on a sec.' He was about to end the call when flickering red lights through the blind caught his attention. He crossed the room and opened the blind again.

'Gotta go, Sal. Talk later.'

Three police cars took off at a rate of knots as he watched, one of them with the siren going.

Something was wrong. Very wrong. Throwing his phone down, Grant raced for the door and flung it open just in time to hear Cathy scream.

He looked up and saw the broken window before he reached her door.

'Bloody hell,' he muttered. Making a fist to pound on the door, he called her name, but the door was flung open and Cathy stood there, her face white and her chest heaving.

She tried to talk, but he couldn't understand her. He grabbed her and held her shoulders firmly. 'Breathe, Cathy, deep breaths and then tell me. What's wrong?'

She nodded and her breath hitched. As she spoke, two policemen hurried around the side of her duplex. 'The window. I heard the window break. I looked out the kitchen window and I saw him. I raced into the kids' room but I was too late.'

She crumpled and fell to her knees as he tried to hold her. 'They're both gone. He's got both my babies. I know it was him. I saw him.'

The police officer closest to them spoke to Grant. 'Can you bring Ms Kendall over to the station? We'll deal with this. He won't be far, and he's on foot.'

'No, I want to help. He told me he'd hurt them if I went to the police; it's all my fault.' Cathy pushed herself to her feet and tried to run, but Grant wrapped her in his arms.

'Sweetheart, the police are on it. Let them go and do their job.'

She tried to pull away and the older policeman mouthed to Grant. 'Paramedic, sedative.'

He nodded and held Cathy tightly. 'Come on, we'll go over to the police station. We can help from there.'

'The river. Go to the river,' she screamed after them. 'He'll take them there, I know he will.'

Grant lifted Cathy into his arms and carried her across the road to the police station.

Chapter 19

The whole night passed in a blur for Cathy. They'd only been at the police station for minutes when the paramedics arrived, and she felt a sharp prick in her arm. She was conscious but she watched the events of the night unfold through a dreamy fog state; she knew something was very wrong, but she couldn't remember what it was.

Grant held her tightly and spoke to people who came and went, but it was all a blur. Time slowed and then went fast as she watched first the policemen, and then many other people come and go. Ryan and Joe, Stavros Levonis, Hunter Sullivan and then Dodge Myers.

Edwina Lette walked past with a tray of teacups followed closely by Esther Ainslie.

It must be a party, but why were they having it at the police station? She smiled at Jaclyn as her friend sat beside her and put her arm around Cathy's shoulder and then Grant moved away from her.

She tried to call him back, but her mouth was full of cotton wool. He turned around as she lifted her hand to call him and then he came back and kissed her hard.

In front of everyone.

'Look after her, Jaclyn,' she heard him say

188

as her hearing cleared for a moment.

Cathy wanted to smile but knew she wasn't supposed to.

And then she was dreaming when Lea and David walked into the room with Cleo.

Oh dear, what if Russ had been invited too? She really didn't want that.

Lea sat on her other side and put her head against Cathy's, and her cheeks were wet,

She tried to say, 'Don't cry, Lea,' but the room spun, and she knew it was time to go to sleep.

***

Joe and Ryan headed to the river with Grant. He'd asked the co-ordinator of the search parties, Senior Constable Taylor, which areas of the river bank had been allocated and Abby told them to go west. The night was hot and steamy, and they were quiet as they ran up Court Street past River Cottage. Torches flickered in the backyard, and Ryan ran across to check it was one of the search parties. He gave a thumbs up and ran back to them.

'From now on, keep an eye out for either of the kids. Potter's hurt so there's no way he could carry both of them as far as the river.'

They ran through the caravan park, checking dark corners and verandas as they passed the cabins and then headed along the riverbank towards the bridge that crossed the river on Mount

Ingalls Road. 'I'll take this side, you both cross the bridge and take the Boggabri side of the river,' Grant said.

Ryan and Joe took off towards the road to get to the bridge, and Ryan flashed his light at the reeds along the bank of the river. He stopped as there was a rustling sound and then a splash in front of him. He watched but it was only some sort of nocturnal animal crossing the river.

Grant was about to move off when a quiet rustle caught his attention. He walked ahead about twenty-five metres, deliberately flashing his torch left and right and when he reached a stand of weeping willows, he switched his flashlight off and silently doubled back further away from the bank. He reached the point where he'd heard the noise and stood silently, listening. He was soon rewarded by a small cry.

Making his way quietly closest to the river, he spotted a flash of white and risked turning his flashlight on.

Billy was lying on his back, blood coming from his nose. Grant slid down the bank and crouched beside him.

'Billy, it's me, Grant. Where are you hurt?'

Billy was in the water up to his knees and he started to cry when he realised it was Grant.

'He took Josie, he was going to throw her in

the river, so I tripped him and he dropped her and he swore, and then he punched my face.'

'Where did Josie go. Which way?'

'Up towards the bridge, but he ran after her. Go and find her, Grant, she's not a very good swimmer.'

'Good man. Can you crawl into the long reeds there and keep very, very quiet? I'll come back for you as soon as I find Josie.'

Billy snuffled and nodded. 'I can.'

'Totally quiet, mate. Make it hard for even me to find you. Get deep into those reeds.'

Grant pulled his phone out of his pocket and dialled Ryan.

'Grant?'

'I've found Billy,' he said quietly as he pushed along the edge of the water. His shoes were hindering his progress, so he took them off along with his socks. 'He's okay and hiding. Potter's headed towards the bridge. He's chasing Josie, she got away from him, so be careful. I'm only fifty metres away from the bridge.'

Grant made one more call back to Abby Taylor and filled her in.

'Roger, got that,' she said quickly. 'I'll divert every search party to the Mt Ingalls Road bridge.' Grant had just put his phone back in his pocket when something hard slammed into his back, and almost knocked him off his feet. He regained his balance and held his light up just as Mike Potter swung a timber post at him for the second time. He ducked, and the momentum of his swing threw Potter off his feet and he landed on his back, dropping the post in the wet shingle.

Grant picked up the timber post, stood over the thug and pressed it hard into the man's blood-soaked chest. 'Where are they, you bastard?' He wasn't going to let on he'd come across Billy.

'Chucked 'em both in the river. Sunk like bloody stones, they did. The bitch mother will get what she deserves. I told her not to call the bloody police.'

'You're a liar, Potter.'

Sirens sounded as the police cars tore along River Road, and Ryan flashed his light in a high arc. It was only a matter of minutes before Potter was handcuffed.

'I need the ambos,' he screamed. 'This bloke attacked me with a timber post. I was just out looking for those missing kids.'

'Try it on, mate. You're going down for a lot of years.' The policeman turned to Grant. 'Great work. I'm AJ. Where are the kids?'

'Billy's back there hiding in the reeds. Josie took off, but this mongrel says he threw her in the river.'

'Right, I'll get Abby to get some lights down here too.' He put his hand on Grant's shoulder. 'Don't worry, we'll find her.'

Chapter 20

Every able-bodied man and woman, as well as the entire Bindarra Creek constabulary, plus a large contingent of police from Tamworth, searched the river until dawn.

Grant was soaking wet and exhausted, but he hadn't taken a break in eight hours. The sky was beginning to lighten to the east as he and Joe made their way to the section of the river that wound past the brewery. This was the furthest they'd been down the Akuna River, and it had wound past many deep holes. The river was flowing fast around this bend, and he felt sick to the stomach at the thought of Josie being carried along by the current until she couldn't stay above water any longer.

The sky quickly lightened from pale apricot to pink and soon as daylight approached, it turned a pale blue.

'We're going to have to go back, mate,' Joe said as they approached a section of the river where the banks were thickly timbered. 'We can't get past here.'

'I'm not going back to Cathy without Josie,' Grant said adamantly. 'I couldn't bear to look at her face when she realises I've let her down.'

Joe's hand touched his shoulder. 'Sit down for a while. We'll take a breather and then work our way through that as far as we can.'

Grant was starting to imagine coming across a little lifeless body, and he kept his eyes open to stop the image from forming in his thoughts. They sat there for ten minutes, both of them constantly scanning the bank on the other side.

'We'd better call in, in case there's news.'

Grant shook his head. 'They would have called us. Okay, you call and ask how Cathy and Billy are.'

He pushed himself to his feet and walked along the river as Joe made the call.

Grant kept his eyes down and he stopped suddenly as he spotted what looked like a small footprint in the shingle.

Not wanting to get his or Joe's hopes up, he walked along until he reached the indentation. His heart started pumping furiously as he saw the track of small footprints leading into the thick scrub ahead.

He stopped and took a breath as light-headedness threatened. Joe was approaching behind him as Grant hurried into the dark shadows of the sheltering bush.

He kept his eyes on the ground and realised that the footprints had disappeared. He stopped and pulled out his flashlight as he searched around, but they simply stopped at the base of a large tree.

Hope flooded through him as he swung the light up into the low foliage and it flashed on something white. He pulled himself up onto the lower branches and began to climb. The bush rustled as Joe followed him into the low scrub. About five metres from the ground, a wide and almost flat branch came out from the centre trunk

Josie was fast asleep above him in the small hollow where the branch joined the trunk.

Grant pulled himself higher until his head was level with the branch. Moisture stung his eyes as he reached out and gently touched her face. Her skin was warm, her face pink and her little chest rose evenly as she slept. Her clothes were wet, and her damp hair was stuck to the sides of her face and neck.

Grant quickly climbed back down. There was no point disturbing her until help was on the way.

His words choked as Joe approached. Grant tried to talk, failed and then started again. 'She's alive. Up the tree, tucked in a hollow and sound asleep. Can you go out on the road and call for help? We'll need an ambulance.'

Joe was off like a shot, his phone to his ear, and Grant could hear his footsteps thudding through the bush.

He climbed up again quietly, looking for the best way to bring her down.

Josie stirred when he gently touched her hand. 'Wake up, sweetie, I'm going to take you home to Mummy and Billy.'

Her little mouth opened in an O of surprise and then her eyes clouded. 'Has the nasty man gone again? He was really cranky when I ran away. I kicked his legs and he fell over and I hid for a while. He was silly. He went the wrong way so I ran this way.'

'You, young lady, are the cleverest and bravest girl I have ever met. Your mum is going to be so happy to see you, and so proud of you.'

'Did Billy get away too?'

'He did. He's back with your mum. Now, do you think you can sit up and put your arms around my neck, and hang on real tight?'

Josie sat up and nodded.

Grant turned his back to her, and she did as he asked.

He turned and hugged the trunk as he carefully climbed down. 'Hang on tight.'

'I am. You know where I got the idea to hide in the tree?' she asked in a conversational tone.

'No, where did you? From a movie?'

'No, from the book I was reading when he

broke our window. It was about a magical treehouse.'

Josie kept chatting with him as they reached the ground and headed for River Road. Grant nodded as she spoke to him.

He almost fell over as they approached the road. In the distance, he could see a police car and an ambulance.

'You know what, Grant?' Josie said in her conversational tone. 'I think you'd make a pretty good dad. Billy and I need one, you know.'

He grinned as he answered. 'I think you'd better talk to your mum about that. And look, I can see her coming now.'

Cathy held her arms open as she ran along the last twenty metres of the track towards them. Her arms went around Josie, and she smothered her daughter's face with kisses before she reached up and kissed Grant's mouth.

'Thank you, Grant. I owe you so much. Abby told me you wouldn't give up.'

Josie's elbow nudged Grant in the side. 'That's a yes, Grant,' she said.

Epilogue
Cathy

The forensic investigation results came in much more quickly than anyone anticipated. The parents of Jilly Baxter, the missing backpacker had provided DNA and there was a result within three weeks. They were coming over to hold a service in a few weeks, and to take their daughter home.

Coupled with the information that Billy and Josie had both given independently to the Tamworth detectives that Potter had told them he was going to drown them both and bury them in a hole like he'd buried another girl, was enough for Potter to be charged with murder and two counts of attempted murder.

Russ Kendall had been extradited to New South Wales and had been cleared of any involvement in the girl's murder, but had been charged with the robbery. On top of his current charge sheet, he too, was going to spend quite a long time in prison.

Cathy had told the kids they had a big half-brother and Grant had brought Sally and Beau over for a visit. The visit had gone well, and Beau was going to start a traineeship with Grant. He was yet to meet Lea and David, but they were keen to meet their new grandson.

The counsellor the kids had been seeing had advised that Cathy spend some time with the children near the river, so it didn't build up in their minds as a place to be scared.

On a Saturday afternoon early in December, Cathy and Grant sat on a blanket on the grass watching Billy and his friend, Eddie Taylor, in their kayaks. Josie was paddling in the shallows.

'As soon as they knew Potter was going to be locked up, they both made an amazing recovery,' Cathy said as she watched Josie. Grant was keeping a very close eye on the boys. The river was running but they were fine if they stayed close to the bank out of the current.

'They make me feel inadequate,' she added.

'Cathy, anyone who went through what you did, and went back to normality the next day is not inadequate,' Grant said, putting his arm around her shoulder.

Cathy leaned back against him and smiled when his lips nuzzled her neck. She was totally relaxed with Grant now and had to assure him daily that what was developing quickly between them was not based on gratitude.

She'd worried about Lea and David's reaction, but they'd been really happy for them.

Grant must have read her mind. 'Do you

think Lea and David would like to have the kids for a weekend? We could go down to the coast and drop them off and finally have that dinner date you promised me,' he said. 'Would you feel safe if they were with their grandparents?'

'I think that sounds like a really good plan. Josie really misses her Nan and Pa.' Cathy chuckled. 'Billy's too busy growing up. He could take his kayak. Lea said the river down there is clear and calm.'

'And you'd be happy to leave them for a night? We can get two rooms if you want.'

Cathy tipped her head back and fluttered her eyelashes at this man she was really starting to care for deeply. 'Now why would you want to waste good money on two rooms?'

'Just checking,' he said kissing her neck again. 'I've seen how much you like to save since you started work.'

Cathy had started part-time in the office at the school and was getting her application ready for the full-time job. The other days, she was manning the office at Grant's yard.

'Not for much longer. Remember, I'm paying you rent from the New Year.'

'You are not.'

'I am too.'

'No, you're not.'

Before she could reply, Grant's lips covered hers. Cathy closed her eyes; her kids were getting used to seeing their mother soundly kissed.

'Get a room, you two,' Billy called out across the water.

Cathy pulled away and waved to her son. 'Billy Kendall, don't be rude. Your sister is too young to hear things like that.'

Josie skipped up to them. 'Grant, speaking of rooms, did you think any more about what I said the day you rescued me from my magical tree?'

Cathy narrowed her eyes and looked at Josie. 'What scheme are you cooking up now, Josie?'

'Nothing, Mummy. Just a plan that Grant and I discussed. I'm sure he'll ask you soon, won't you Grant?'

Cathy looked at Grant and then at Josie. 'Why, Grant Cummings,' she said with a chuckle. 'I think my daughter has made you blush. I'll look forward to hearing about this plan.'

'Not too soon, Josie,' Grant said. 'I want to give you all time to get used to me.'

'Does that mean you've decided to stay in Bindarra Creek, Grant?' Cathy asked, her tone serious.

'Are you going to stay in Bindarra Creek, Cathy?' His tone matched hers.

'If you are, I am.' She reached up and kissed him again. Josie rolled her eyes and ran down to the water.

'Are you, Grant?' Cathy asked again

'I am. I've made my peace with this town, and I can see myself living here for a long time, as long as a certain beautiful lady is happy to have me living here.'

'She is very happy with that plan.'

'Then I'll start working on Josie's plan,' he said.

'Are you going to tell me what it is?' Cathy asked.

'She invited me to be their dad. When the time is right, you and I will talk about it.'

Cathy nodded. 'We will.'

There were no more rude comments from Billy or Josie as Grant kissed her thoroughly.

THE END

For your reading pleasure, here is an excerpt from the next book in the Bindarra Creek Mystery Series:
Forgotten Secrets © Susanne Bellamy

Chapter 1

Thunder rumbled through the hills of the national park, echoes bouncing off steep granite walls as the storm rolled towards Bindarra Creek. Seth Gordon stood on the veranda of his farmhouse and scanned the back paddock all the way down to the short drop to the riverbank. The Akuna River was flowing higher than usual and the first day of summer promised more rain, and further flooding.

Banjo, six-months-old and as curious as Kelpie-Border Collie cross puppies were, had nosed his way through the loose mesh screen of the kitchen door. It wouldn't be so bad except . . . Seth sniffed the air. The hairs on his neck prickled as he looked from the rushing Akuna River around the empty house yard and green paddock.

La Ninã had more than compensated for years of drought. The regional dam had released water twice in the past three months, but the clouds were as dark as the granite cliffs in the national park across the river.

Lightning flashed, eerie behind the misty veil of heavy-bellied clouds. More rain was on the way and Banjo hated storms.

'Banjo! Here, boy.' Seth waited for a yipping tan and gold streak to rush towards him. When seconds passed and Banjo failed to appear, Seth checked beneath the veranda then jogged across the yard and pushed headfirst between thick bushes planted by his grandmother over fifty years earlier.

'Come on, little fella. It will be dry and warm inside.'

Twigs caught his hair, and a leaf tickled the inside of his ear as he scanned the low spaces beneath the bushes. Fixing the screen door so the pup couldn't nose it open jumped to the top of his long list. So many jobs Gramps hadn't been able to stay on top of towards the end of his life. Now, the list was Seth's to tackle.

He backed out of the bushes and called again.

A high-pitched whine was drowned out by another roll of thunder, but now, with an idea of where it came from, Seth made his way down the slope. His gaze fixed on the rotting, rusty, iron-roofed kennel he'd meant to break up for firewood and replace.

As he bent down to peer inside, Banjo's nose poked through the opening, and a small, pink tongue licked his chin.

'Come out of there, you little rascal.' Seth tucked the pup into the crook of his arm and stroked his head. 'Let's get you something to eat and curl up in front of the fire.'

The dull roar of a plane flying low over the national park drew his gaze to the sky. Silver, white and blue flashed in a brief break between the clouds.

'Bad weather to be flying in.' He tickled the pup under the chin then stroked his head and looked back along the river towards town. Water churned around a rocky outcrop to the west and Seth's gaze narrowed. Had the water level risen again?

Movement caught his eyes. Something white had fallen out of the clouds, growing larger as it fell towards the river.

That was a parachute!

Why would anyone parachute in this weather?

As he watched, the chute spiralled down and disappeared behind the row of trees that marked his boundary with *Craigellachie*, Angus McGregor's property.

Drawn down the slope by curiosity, Seth

spotted an Icarus-sized splash in the Akuna River. A parachute spun gracefully before settling across the surface like a sheet. Greedy water sucked at it.

Where's the parachutist?

Even as the thought formed, he set Banjo on the ground and ran. The river was running high, and the current was strong, but still, the jumper should have surfaced unless . . .

Toeing off his boots and dragging his shirt over his head, Seth scanned the water around the floating parachute.

There!

A head bobbed to the surface, but the parachutist was making no effort to swim or to free himself from the chute.

Seth raced along the bank and dived into the water, swimming hard towards the blonde head. He was a few strokes from the body when it sank. Taking a deep breath, he dived, lunging underwater, reaching out and – *relief* – grabbing a handful of clothing and harness.

His lungs burned as he kicked hard, dragging the limp body to the surface. Had he got to them in time?

His head broke the surface, and he shifted the person's head onto his shoulder then felt for a pulse.

Thank God – no need for mouth-to-mouth.

A woman floated in his arms, her eyes closed. Blood flowed from a wound on her temple, and the river clutched at her like a living creature, tugging her parachute and trying to drag her under.

Seth's muscles strained as he fought to keep her head above water and struggled to open the harness. It wouldn't budge. Already the river had carried them halfway along his property's frontage. Giving up on the harness, he stroked at an angle towards the bank. Adrenaline overcame muscle fatigue as he towed the woman to shore. The river would not take her, not on his watch. Shaking his head, he blinked water from his eyes, and searched for a place to land.

Overhead, the sky darkened, and the first plops of rain pitted the river's surface. The powerful current tugged at the woman's chute, but finally, Seth's foot hit a small, rocky bank below the river paddock.

Woman and chute weighed heavy in his arms, but he manhandled her up the drop-off onto the grass and tipped her onto her side in recovery position before falling onto his hands and knees. A trickle of water ran from her mouth.

Seth's chest heaved as he hung his head, dragging in several noisy, gasping breaths. When he could speak, he tapped her cheek and said, 'Hey, can you hear me?'

She didn't respond.

He checked her pulse. Strong, if a bit fast.

The rain was becoming heavier, not yet stinging his bare skin, but green-tinged clouds threatened hail. He had to get the woman inside.

The harness clip still refused to open. Turning his attention to the tangled strings of the parachute, he delved into his pocket for his Swiss Army knife. His hand came out empty and he groaned. Lost to the river, he guessed. Gathering the lines, he hauled the rest of the chute ashore. Having rescued the woman from the water's clutches, he wasn't about to let the river pull her back in.

A familiar, drumming noise impinged on his hearing. The raindrops grew heavier and suddenly, the leading edge of the storm hit them. Stinging, heavy rain with small hailstones. Swearing, Seth grabbed an armful of parachute under one arm and tossed the woman over his shoulder. Body aching as he jogged up the paddock, he called Banjo to follow. For once, the pup obeyed, lolloping beside him up to the farmhouse.

Breathing hard, he dropped the chute at the top of the stairs and lowered the woman against the wall, but the noise was deafening. Hail bounced and he flinched when a piece hit his cheek. Blast it, they needed to be inside.

The parachute trailed like a bridal train

down the back stairs.

Wiping water from his eyes and face, he wrenched the kitchen door open. Banjo raced through ahead of him. Seth grabbed a kitchen knife and, returning to the woman, cut the harness off. Leaving the mess of silk and tangled lines and the knife where they lay, he carried the woman into the lounge room and set her down on the sofa. The room was warm with a low fire burning in the grate, but both he and the stranger were soaked. Water puddled around his knees, and he grimaced as Gran's favourite chintz covering darkened around the woman's body.

Sorry, Gran.

Seth pulled the knee rug from the back of the sofa. Hoping the smell of river water didn't obliterate the faint hint of Gran's violet perfume that clung to the wool, he tucked the zigzag-patterned rug under the stranger's shoulders. Gran had made the rug for him back when he was a little kid. He'd made it into a fort, and he'd wrapped it around himself in the middle of winter then sat staring into the leaping flames of the fire.

And now it covered this stranger he'd pulled out of the Akuna River.

Goosebumps rose on his bare arms. Only now they were out of immediate danger and with the luxury of a blazing fire did he realise he was shivering, but the woman's face was pale. Warming her was more important than his own comfort.

Banjo plopped his head and two front paws on Seth's calf and whimpered.

'It's okay, Banjo. You're safe in here.' He patted the quivering puppy and tossed a large cushion onto the floor in front of the fire. The pup snuggled into the soft depths and closed his eyes.

The fire was burning low, so Seth threw several small logs on and poked them until the flames drew taller and brighter. Once he was satisfied with the heat it pumped out, he knelt beside the woman and smoothed her hair from her face.

She was perhaps in her late twenties, slim, with fair skin that looked as though she spent more time indoors than outside, and her clothes looked expensive, though what did Seth know.

'Hello, can you hear me?' He checked her pulse. It was stronger than before, better than he'd expected after her ditching in the river. Tapping her cheek lightly, he repeated the question.

Blonde hair lay plastered to her scalp and her skin was cool, but her breathing was regular. If only she would wake, he'd feel better.

His phone was on the kitchen bench, alongside his first aid kit. He grabbed both, thumbing the phone on and punching in 000 as he headed towards the lounge room door. Lightning flashed, making the kitchen brighter than day, and thunder cracked overhead. Then the kitchen light flickered and went out, plunging the room behind him into thick greyness. The lightning must have made a direct hit on the power lines and the emergency number failed to connect.

Seth entered the lounge room and dropped the phone onto the arm of the sofa. First things first. He put on the headlamp he'd added as a standard item to his first aid kit and set about examining the woman's head wound.

Two deep, thin, parallel cuts on her temple seeped blood into her hair, and the beginning of a large bruise discoloured the surrounding skin. He cleaned and dressed the wound while considering what could have caused such cuts. Deep and straight, he thought possibly contact with a metal door frame.

One thing he was certain of; the wound wasn't from her dunking in the river, so it must have happened either before or as she jumped.

Only one plane had passed overhead before he spotted her chute.

Focusing on that memory, he sifted through what he recalled. It had a white and blue fuselage and was possibly a Cessna 208. His glimpse had been brief, but combined with the sound of the engine, he thought that most likely. Perhaps it would be enough to reunite her with friends or family, whoever she'd been flying with before her jump. When the power returned and he had mobile service, a call to CASA might find planes that had logged a flight plan over Bindarra Creek around . . . He checked the time. After four p.m., so the plane must have been overhead no later than a quarter to the hour.

He glanced through the window. Despite the fact it was early summer, and barely after four o'clock, the room was dark, but the hail was lessening. Once he'd cleaned then taped a surgical pad in place over the woman's head wound, Seth ran his hands over her arms and then her legs. As he reached her right ankle, his hands stilled.

She's wearing one stiletto shoe.

He kneeled beside her, fixated on the oddity. Nobody went parachuting wearing stilettos. He lifted the blanket and frowned. He needed to remove her wet clothes, which were what his cousin, Sonya would have called 'upmarket office chic'.

Gently, he slipped an arm under the woman's neck and removed the slim-fitting cream jacket from her shoulders. Even to his untrained eye, more used to farmer's beige or army green, the jacket looked expensive, and her blouse was . . .

Given it had been soaked in brown river water, his best guess was pale lemon silk. He bet not even a city drycleaner could bring it back after its encounter with the Akuna River.

Before he removed her blouse and a pair of black leather trousers that fit her like a second skin, he pulled the blanket over her then slipped into his bedroom and rummaged through his chest of drawers. Dragging out an old T-shirt, soft after many washes, and his flannelette PJs, he figured she would be warm, if swamped by his clothes.

He stripped off his sodden T-shirt and jeans and pulled on a grey sweatshirt and trackpants. Slipping his feet into his Ugg boots, he returned to the woman, grabbing a towel and another blanket from the linen cupboard on his way.

She hadn't moved.

Unbuttoning the many pearl buttons tried his patience, but finally her shirt slid open, and he peeled it off, revealing an ivory lace bra.

He called up the instructor's voice from his early training sessions after he joined the Army Reserve Field Hospital: *Treat the patient with respect and dignity, but don't get hung up if you have to undress them. Got it?*

Got it, he reminded himself.

Rubbing her chilled skin vigorously with the towel until colour returned, it was easier to then slip dry clothing on than removing her wet things had been. Soon, he had dressed her in warm clothing and covered her with both blankets. When he'd done all he could to make her comfortable, he sat in the armchair and leaned his head against the high back. Set at a right angle between the sofa and the fire, he watched her for signs of regaining consciousness.

Minutes passed as three questions buzzed in his brain: Why was his patient dressed in city clothing, in *stilettoes* even, for a parachute jump? What had caused her head injury? Why had she jumped from a plane during a storm?

Shaking his head, he gathered her wet clothes and headed to the laundry to hang them to drip dry. As he lifted the hangers onto the drying railing, his shoulder muscles twinged. Maybe a shot of whisky was in order to warm the cockles of his heart, as Gran used to say. Just one though. The night could be long if the woman didn't wake.

He set a dram of whisky in a cut-glass tumbler on the inlaid table beside his armchair, but the mystery of the woman's arrival nagged at him. He drank half his drink, relishing the warmth sliding down his throat. Seth didn't like mysteries.

Tossing back the rest of his whisky, he went out the back and hauled her parachute onto the veranda. The lines were a mess, but that could be attributed to the action of the water and his dragging the whole lot up the back paddock, so he set about examining the chute itself. Metres and metres of sodden fabric passed through his hands.

Just what he was looking for he wasn't sure. As he was about to give up and call himself all kinds of fool, his finger slipped through a hole.

A hole that, to his army-trained eye, was familiar.

A perfectly round hole that had no business being where it was.

A bullet hole.

BUY FORGOTTEN SECRETS NOW

A Bindarra Creek Mystery Romance Series – released from July 2022

Amulet of Death – Suzanne Gilchrist (aka E.E. Gilchrist)
Beyond the Gate – Rhonda Forrest
Protecting Their Destiny – Erin Moira O'Hara
Only She Knew – Linda Charles
Secrets of River Cottage – Annie Seaton
Forgotten Secrets – Susanne Bellamy
A Perfect Danger – Phillipa Nefri Clark

About the Bindarra Creek Series

Welcome to Bindarra Creek, a struggling country town where people work hard and love deeply. Set in the picturesque tablelands of New England, Australia, Bindarra Creek is a fictional, rural community full of romance, intrigue, adventure, drama and suspense.

To date there are four multi-author 'series' set in the Bindarra Creek world all written by best-selling Australian romance authors. A fifth is planned for late 2022 **– A Bindarra Creek Christmas.**

Bindarra Creek A Town Reborn

Take Me Home – Suzanne Gilchrist (aka S E Gilchrist)
In the Heat of the Night – Susanne Bellamy
No Looking Back - Linda Charles
Worth the Wait – Annie Seaton
With Every Breath – Lauren K. McKellar
Stealing Her Heart – Simone Angela
A Twist of Fate – Erin Moira O'Hara
Promise Me Forever – Juanita Kees

Bindarra Creek Short & Sweet

What's in a Kiss – Linda Charles
My Forever Valentine – Sandie James (not available)
Pearls and Green Beer – Susanne Bellamy
Full Circle – Annie Seaton
Date with Destiny – Erin Moira O'Hara
A Letter From the Queen – Lee Christine
Love's Sweet Challenge – Suzanne Gilchrist (aka S E Gilchrist)
The Widow Maker – Lauren K. McKellar
Out of the Blue – Noelle Clark

Bindarra Creek Romance

Bindarra Creek Makeover - S. E. Gilchrist
Shadows of the Heart - Lee Christine

Second Chance Love - Susanne Bellamy
The CEO Mechanic - Sandie James (not available)
Reach for the Stars - Kerrie Paterson
Home to Bindarra Creek - Juanita Kees
Stolen Sanctuary - Stacey Nash
Tempting Fate - Erin Moira O'Hara
One More Day - Linda Charles
The Vine - Lauren K. McKellar
The Ghost of His Past - Simone Angela
Joanie's Dilemma - Marianne Theresa
Buckley's Chance - Noelle Clark
Full details on buy links for all books in Bindarra Creek world can be found at:
www.bindarracreekromance.com

Thank you for reading Secrets of River Cottage.

Below you will find an extract from my latest release, *East of Alice.*

PROLOGUE

Ethan had asked her to help paint his Land Rover the week before she'd started at Charles Darwin Uni in Alice. He'd used Mum's good vacuum cleaner switched to reverse, reading out the instructions he'd found on YouTube. 'Fit the hose into the blow of the vacuum. Turn on the vacuum, and place your finger on the hole on top of the spray jar to start spraying.'

They'd been weak from laughter by the time the paint job had been finished. Then, when it was dry, Ethan had hand-painted the wheel hubs black with a paintbrush.

He'd surveyed their handiwork. 'Looks bloody shit, doesn't it, Gem?'

Gemma could only nod. Not the best job, by a long shot.

'I won't get lost in Ruby anyway,' he'd said as they'd scrubbed paint off the driveway.

That had been the last time they'd done something together.

By the time Mum had discovered the ruined vacuum, Ethan had headed off, and Gemma had borne the brunt of her temper.

It was another two weeks before they'd started to worry. Ethan had done his own thing in those days, staying away from home a lot because Mum was always on his case about getting a traineeship or going to uni. But he'd always come home eventually.

Until he didn't.

CHAPTER 1

Alice Springs
27 January

Gemma Hayden stood at the front of her new classroom and drew in a deep breath. It didn't matter where the school was or how new it was, that same familiar smell of a primary school classroom always filled her with happy anticipation. The waxy crayons, the rubber of the kickballs in the storeroom, the mustiness of books, and the oddly pleasant smell of glue all combined to create that unique atmosphere. There were only three days before the school year began, and although the fresh and eager faces staring up at her this year would be unfamiliar, the promise of making a difference in those children's lives dispelled any lingering doubts Gemma held about her move back to the Northern Territory.

Home.

Trephina Primary School was on the eastern side of Alice Springs and close to the Ross Highway, which led out to the East MacDonnell Ranges. She was close enough to Ruby Gap to go out and camp on weekends and holidays—if she wanted to. The old house where Dad's great-grandmother had given birth to two boys over a hundred years ago was in ruins, and the land had since been subsumed by National Parks to create a nature park, but Dad had always made sure that she and Ethan knew where their family had come from.

Crossing to the window, Gemma stared across the grey asphalt of the playground to the east, where the range beckoned. The low mountains might look smoky blue from a distance, but she knew that the dramatic ridges and bluffs were a deep ochre and red, broken only by stands of white ghost gums marking dry stream beds. She and Ethan had spent much of their childhood at Ruby Gap, fossicking for gemstones, listening to Dad's yarns and surviving his ordinary camp cooking. Despite his basic cooking skills, he'd taught them both how to survive in the harsh Australian bush, the tricks to finding water, and the bush tucker you could find if you knew where to look.

Gemma opened the equipment cupboard and tried to stop her thoughts being pulled down into the dark past. She had clung to hope for a long time, and maybe it was time to accept her brother was not coming back. Maybe her mother was right; maybe she shouldn't have come back to the Territory.

She shook her head; her happy mood had evaporated. She'd come back to the school tomorrow and finish her inventory. She closed the cupboard, resting her head against the doors. 'Where are you, Ethan?' she whispered.

'Who are you?' Gemma jumped at the gruff voice and turned to see a woman with tightly permed grey hair framing an unfriendly face furrowed with deep wrinkles.

'I'm the new Year Two teacher. Gemma Hayden.' She crossed the room to stand beside the newcomer and tried not to wrinkle her nose at the strong smell of smoke emanating from her clothes. 'Can I help you?'

The woman nodded and looked her up and down, unsmiling. 'You're a bit early for term, aren't you? I'm Pat Turner, the head cleaner. I don't let the teachers come in this week. How did you get the key?'

She doesn't let them? Gemma raised her eyebrows and stared back. 'Jeff gave it to me. The principal. Along with his permission to come in this week.' As soon as she justified her presence in the school, she was angry with herself that she'd found it necessary.

'I know who Jeff Thompson is.'

'I imagine you do.' Gemma couldn't help the coolness in her voice. If there was one thing she wouldn't tolerate, it was bullying and this woman was trying it on.

'So, are you going now?'

Even though Gemma had been about to leave, there was no way this woman was going to harass her out of her own classroom. 'No, I have a few more things to do. I'll be here a while yet.'

Pat folded her arms and sat on the edge of one of the low tables. 'I'll wait here until you're done. We're going to polish the floors in these rooms this afternoon. There's a mess of paint on the floor in the wet room. I hope you've got more control over the kids than the last one.'

'There's no need for you to wait.' The pursing of the woman's mouth reminded Gemma of her mother and that made her all the more determined not to be bullied. The days of being cajoled into doing what everyone else wanted were long gone. She held her gaze steady. 'I'll let you know when I'm finished.'

The woman shook her head. 'Jeff had no right to give you a key. You don't officially start until Monday.'

A great start to my time at Trephina. Then common sense kicked in; there was no point pushing the issue. If there was one thing Gemma had learned about the politics of schools over the past three years, it was the importance of keeping the cleaners on side.

'Okay. I'll get out of your way.' Gemma forced a smile, keeping her voice sweet. 'My preparation will have to wait. It was good to meet you, Pat.'

The woman's eyes widened as she stood. 'Hang on … Gemma Hayden? You related to Ethan Hayden?'

A tremble ran through Gemma and she lifted her chin. 'Why do you ask?'

'He was good mates with my Jed.' For the first time Pat's face lost its belligerence. 'You're his sister? You look like him. Twins, weren't you?'

'Yes, we are.' Gemma's interest quickened. 'I didn't know Ethan had a mate called Jed. Did the police talk to him back then?'

Pat shook her head. 'I don't know. Jed—the boys called him Screw—had already gone to work on a cattle station in the East Kimberley when I heard Ethan went missing.'

'Oh, I remember Screw!' Ethan, Screw and Saul Pearce had been tight from their first day at high school. They used to do everything together, and Gemma had been terribly jealous. They were allowed to go bush and she hadn't been allowed to tag along. Her dad had allowed Ethan to go because Saul was a couple of years older, but Gemma had long suspected he hadn't wanted his little girl camping in the outback. 'How is he?'

'He hung around for a while when you all left school, then took off to Roselyon.'

'Where's Roselyon?'

'Some bloody huge cattle station near Lake Argyle. You know, that bugger hasn't been home once since he left. But that's kids for you.' Pat's tone was friendlier. 'So, you're a local girl, hey? The school community'll like that.'

'I am. It's good to be home.'

'Come outside with me, love. We can chat while I have a smoke.'

Gemma picked up her bag and followed Pat outside. 'Where are you living? Your parents aren't here anymore, are they?'

'No. Dad lives in Darwin. I moved to the east coast with Mum when they split up, and I finished my teaching degree there. I've got an apartment out near the university now.'

Once they settled on one of the box seats surrounding a pretty garden with a small lemon tree in the middle, Pat lit up. 'Move further up so the smoke won't bother you.' She waved to the far end of the wooden bench.

'No, it's okay.' Gemma didn't care how

much smoke there was if Pat wanted to talk about Ethan. 'So, the police didn't talk to Screw, I mean, Jed, back then?'

'I don't know. I'll be honest with you, we had a blue before he left, and we haven't talked since then. Maybe they did contact him, who knows?'

'So, is he still there?'

'I got a Christmas card from him the second year he was gone, from a cattle station up in the Gulf. Who knows where he is now? Bloody kids. Don't even have his phone number. Never hear much from his sister either. She lives in Cairns. Haven't even met my first grandchild yet.' Pat shrugged.

Gemma gave a sympathetic murmur. 'Do you think Jed might have known something? Did he leave home before Ethan went?'

The woman puffed a cloud of smoke. 'Listen, love, I can't remember what I had for breakfast most days, so I sure as hell ain't going to remember the date he took off. What was it? Five years ago?'

'Six.' Gemma tried to contain her frustration. 'Do you remember my brother? He went to Screw's house—I mean, to your place—a lot when they were at school.'

'Of course I do. The three of them used to

hit the fridge like a plague of locusts. When I'd had enough of them, I'd hunt them off to the Pearce place.'

'I didn't know they went there too. Ethan never said.' Gemma knew her voice was dull. She'd managed to put Saul Pearce out of her mind after he'd left her without a word. Don't think about it now.

Pat nodded. 'Ethan was a good kid. Always polite and knew his pleases and thank-yous.'

'He spent a lot of time away after we turned eighteen, but he always texted me and stayed in touch. Mum used to get really angry with him because he didn't enrol in uni when we left high school. You might remember she was principal at St Mary's.'

'Yeah, I remember your mum,' Pat said, her tone indicating they were not friendly memories.

'I thought he'd gone away to keep the peace, but when he didn't come home and we couldn't contact him, we knew something was wrong,' Gemma blurted, unable to stop herself. 'Even after three months the police refused to list him as officially missing. "Ninety-eight per cent of missing persons turn up, and if they don't, there's a good chance they don't want to be found," they said.' Gemma's voice shook. It was still hard to talk about it. She and Mum rarely did. As for Dad …

'Slack bastards.' Pat put her head back and blew out a stream of smoke.

'They just didn't seem to care. They told Mum he was just another young guy who wanted to get away from home and was probably off working somewhere.' Gemma swallowed and sat up straight. 'I knew there was something wrong. It wasn't like him. Even though he and Mum fought, Eth was thoughtful. He'd never take off without telling us. Dad spent weeks driving around and putting up posters of him and his red Land Rover at every rest stop from here to Western Australia, then Queensland. Not one person ever contacted us.' It had broken Dad, waiting for Ethan to come home.

'I wondered where your dad had gone,' Pat said thoughtfully. 'I used to see Tony at the Gidgeewalla pub. I worked there for years before I got the job here at the school.'

'Mum said she knew Ethan was dead and that he wouldn't come back. That's when Dad took off.' Gemma closed her eyes as she remembered the massive fight she'd had with her mother when Mum had announced they were moving to New South Wales. She'd dragged eighteen-year-old Gemma with her, away from her university course. 'I knew … I mean, I know … I know Ethan's not dead. I'd feel something if he was.' Wouldn't she? He was her twin, after all. Gemma was determined not to give up hope. The sooner she could get out to Ruby Gap, the happier she would be. Her only regret was that she had left it for so long to go back out there.

Pat pushed her cigarette butt into the dirt before leaning down to retrieve it and pop it in her pocket. 'I'm sorry you've been through the wringer, love,' she said kindly. 'Anyway, I'd better get back to work. And listen, if there's anything you need here at the school, you ask me. Okay?'

'Thank you, Pat.' Gemma pulled out her phone. 'Can you tell me the name of the cattle property Jed's at now?'

Pat shrugged. 'The only one I ever knew was the first place he went to. Roselyon.'

Gemma nodded, making a note in her phone. 'Okay, thanks.'

It was a start; she'd see if she could contact the property, and maybe they'd know where Screw had gone. She was not going to give up until she found Ethan.

You can find ***East of Alice*** here:
https://www.annieseaton.net/east-of-alice.html

Other Books by the Author

Whitsunday Dawn
Undara
Osprey Reef
East of Alice (November 2022)

Porter Sisters Series
Kakadu Sunset
Daintree
Diamond Sky
Hidden Valley
Larapinta
Kakadu Dawn(June 2023)

Pentecost Island Series
Pippa
Eliza
Nell
Tamsin
Evie
Cherry
Odessa
Sienna
Tess
Also available in three boxed sets
Books 1-3
Books 4-6
Books 7-10

The Augathella Girls Series
Outback Roads
Outback Sky
Outback Escape
Outback Wind
Outback Dawn
Outback Moonlight
Outback Dust
Outback Hope

Sunshine Coast Series
Waiting for Ana
The Trouble with Jack
Healing His Heart
Sunshine Coast Boxed Set

The Richards Brothers Series
The Trouble with Paradise
Marry in Haste
Outback Sunrise
Richards Brothers Boxed Set

Bondi Beach Love Series
Beach House
Beach Music
Beach Walk
Beach Dreams
The House on the Hill

Second Chance Bay Series
Her Outback Playboy
Her Outback Protector
Her Outback Haven
Her Outback Paradise

The McDougalls of Second Chance Bay Boxed Set

Love Across Time Series
Come Back to Me
Follow Me
Finding Home
The Threads that Bind
Love Across Time 1-4 Boxed Set

Bindarra Creek
Worth the Wait
Full Circle
Secrets of River Cottage

Four Seasons Short and Sweet
Ten Days in Paradise
Follow the Sun

Others
Deadly Secrets
Adventures in Time
Silver Valley Witch
The Emerald Necklace
Christmas with the Boss
Her Christmas Star
An Aussie Christmas Duo (the two Christmas novellas)
A Clever Christmas

About the Author

Annie lives in Australia, on the beautiful north coast of New South Wales. She sits in her writing chair and looks out over the tranquil Pacific Ocean.

She writes contemporary romance and loves telling stories that always have a happily ever after. She lives with her very own hero of many years and they share their home with Toby, the naughtiest dog in the universe, and Barney, the ragdoll puss, who hides when the four grandchildren come to visit.

Stay up to date with her latest releases at her website: http://www.annieseaton.net

Acknowledgements

As always a special thank you to my fabulous editors, Susanne Bellamy and Rhonda Forrest, my eagle-eyed proof-readers, Roby Aiken and Kristen Woolgar.

A special thank you to Suzanne Gilchrist for coming up with the concept of the Bindarra Creek series.